THE WAKEFIELD CURSE

/ / / /

J.R. RAIN
&
MATTHEW S. COX

FOUR ELEMENTS TRILOGY

The Elementalist
The Black Rose
The Wakefield Curse

Published by
Crop Circle Books
212 Third Crater, Moon

Printed in the United States of America.

ISBN- 9781675210741

Chapter One
Probably Not Dead

Anger has helped me deal with many things in life, though not always in the best way.

I had a tendency to get angry fairly often. As a coping mechanism, rage wasn't entirely the worst option. It beat downing half a bottle of whisky every time frustration got the better of me. Sure, allowing myself to fly off the handle could be destructive, though mostly I did a lot of yelling. However, I could get un-angry a whole lot faster than I could sober up.

Now, I'm not saying drinking never happened. Heck, I was no stranger to booze, but it never became a crutch for me. Maybe moderation had been a side effect of living in Shadow Pines. In fact, for all our problems, the town had a surprising lack of alcoholics. Of course, we *used to* have some… but stumbling drunks made easy targets for vampires.

The events of the past few weeks appeared to be converging in a way that signaled a giant raging shitstorm prepared to unload its foul contents all over my home town. After my half-succubus girlfriend, Crystal, and our new werewolf friend, Jackson, helped me wipe out the vampires in Wakefield Manor, I'd expected a revenge attack or all-out war. Eradicating one of the Founding Families just wasn't something people tended to accept in stride, even if they had all been vampires.

Well, all but one.

Only one member of the Wakefield family line remained alive: a ten-year-old girl named Blair. Poor kid. She'd been essentially a prisoner in her own home, held captive by her vampire family who wanted to wait for her eighteenth birthday to make her into a vampire, too. Kind of short-sighted if you asked me. Making the last live person in the family a vampire ended any chance for future Wakefields. I guessed they figured nothing could touch them... so why bother with future generations?

Of course, they hadn't factored in Mother Nature.

And me.

Anyway, between Jackson's initial attack and our raid on the manor last night, about twenty-seven vampires ceased to be, leaving Wakefield Manor a giant ghost house. After a brazen challenge like that, I knew the vampires would enact some kind of revenge. However, it never occurred to me that the undead would target my ex-girlfriend, Sheriff Justine Waters.

Outsiders seldom understood how things really worked in Shadow Pines. American history was full of little towns, frequently in the Frontier West, where one man could hold an alarming amount of power over entire areas. Take, for example, a mining town like Ironside. The family who owned the operation back in the 1800s basically did whatever they wanted. Laws didn't matter when the people enforcing them followed the orders of the man in charge. Folklore told of countless unsavory deeds done by various patriarchs, everything from killing rivals to poisoning miners from a competing company to even murdering mistresses. One old mine boss reportedly kept his pregnant mistress locked up in a boarding house he owned. Fortunately, with the spread of government into the frontier and the evolution of the country into the modern world, that sort of thing mostly faded out in the country as a whole.

Except for Shadow Pines.

Oh, it wasn't as overt as it used to be. The patriarch of a family couldn't still blow a man's head off in broad daylight while everyone in town refused to do anything about it out of fear. However, the Founding Families still ruled over this place like neo-royalty, modern day dukes and duchesses in total control of their families' territory. Rather than getting their hands dirty or hiring enforcers, they controlled things mostly by financial power and legal threats. Of course, every so often, the Founders resorted to the old ways if need be. Arson, bombings, assassinations, and so on continued, though somewhat rarely—until the upsurge in vampires.

Never ones to miss a chance at greater power, the members of the Founding Families allied themselves in varying degrees with the undead. Some, like the Wakefields, didn't care what they had to do in order to ensure their relevance. They fully embraced it, becoming vampires themselves. Other families had a vampire or two among them but fell short of sacrificing the entire family. Yet other families, like the Bradburys, avoided becoming undead while still occasionally working with them or hiring them.

My association with Crystal Bradbury could potentially spell political trouble for her family insofar as their relationship with vampires went. However, I didn't intend to let it become a problem. Mostly because my goal involved the eradication of all vampires from Shadow Pines —or at least the destruction of so many that they would no longer give my little town a per-capita murder rate that made Tijuana Mexico seem like Mayberry.

Anyway, the problem with the Founding Families came from their varying degrees of acceptance toward the undead. Nothing hap-pened in Shadow Pines without the approval— or at least tacit permission—of the big nine families. As most of them had become politically involved with vampires, my going up against the undead would make me a threat to those groups. Bad enough the vamps would be coming after me, if the Families got involved, I'd have to worry about normal hitmen, too.

I banked on the hope that if no one had vampires in their pocket, the Families would have no reason to stay pissed off at me since I wouldn't be acting specifically against or for certain families. According to Crystal, a couple of them—namely the Darceys and the Anworths —wanted nothing to do with vampires at all. It weakened them significantly, rendering them nearly irrelevant in local politics for the last few years. Crystal's mother was a Darcey, so she shared their distaste for the undead. Even if Crystal hadn't been part fey, she'd have inherited her familial opinion of them, too. That her very blood contained the opposite energy to vampires changed distaste into loathing.

In addition to infiltrating the local 'royalty,' the undead had influenced my former girlfriend, the sheriff. This enabled them to murder with near impunity since the police would cover everything up and call it an animal attack. Somehow, the extreme number of missing persons cases going on around here attracted *more* tourists, mostly people who'd convinced themselves the stories had all been made up for publicity. We also got a fair amount of 'cryptozoologists' who came here to prove to the world we had a Bigfoot problem since many vampire attacks happened out in the woods to unsuspecting hikers and campers. Outsiders enjoyed a certain degree of protection from vampiric predation—at least in terms of murder. I suspected that whoever pulled the strings of the vampires didn't want the state police or FBI getting involved. If too many out of state tourists kept dropping dead when they came here, that would generate attention of the wrong kind.

Granted, the news hadn't been entirely bleak as of late. A young woman who'd come to me as an 'almost-vampire' walked out the door this morning once again a normal person—with her werewolf boyfriend. We'd managed to destroy the old vampire who turned her into one of the undead before she damned herself by murdering someone and the curse took full hold. Every now and then, a PI caught a case that could make them smile every time they thought about it. Tracy Randall was that case for me. The look of such pure happiness on her face the instant she realized she'd escaped the curse would stay with me for the rest of my life.

Unfortunately, the good vibes didn't last long.

No, nothing bad happened to Tracy that I knew about. One of the sheriff's deputies, Aaron Wilson, stormed into my office not long after the lovebirds left. My former girlfriend had gone missing, and naturally, Aaron suspected me. The end of my relationship with Justine hadn't been the smoothest of things, though no violence had ever been involved between us, merely a lot of shouting. I couldn't quite say in complete truthfulness I had nothing to do with her apparent abduction, even though I'd only found out about it this morning.

Justine had been under some degree of mental control. A couple days ago, I blew her mind by demonstrating the elemental magic

Nature gave me in front of her as well as forcing her to think about the inherent conflict between her duty as sheriff, who she was as a person, and what the compulsion forced her to do. Somewhere in that mess, her mind cracked. Not in a 'going insane' sort of way, but the supernatural influence slipped its grip on her head.

Most logical people would not have blamed me at all for her abduction, but that didn't stop me from feeling guilty. Of course, I hadn't played a direct part in said abduction, merely broke her free from the vampires' control, which made her less useful to them. She'd gone from being their tool to a piece of bait they could dangle to get at me.

Predictably, Deputy Aaron Wilson hadn't been too open to the idea of vampires.

In the interest of avoiding a confrontation with him and/or becoming a sitting duck in a holding cell while he investigated, I decided to bring Aaron up to date on the world of things that shouldn't exist. After a brief display of lightning and fire, he'd stepped back from his accusation enough to listen to me. The man still didn't fully believe what I told him, but he had no easy way to dismiss watching me conjure literal magic in my hands.

He did, however, appear to believe I had

nothing to do—directly—with Justine's disappearance. They hadn't been working on any cases involving big money corporations or organized crime or anything the Founding Families would care about enough to get involved, so Aaron couldn't come up with any more mundane explanations for who would want to grab Justine in the middle of the night. Having no alternative theories to counter my vampire story, he agreed that the best thing we could do was try to find her before dark.

We hopped in his Sheriff's Department Chevy Tahoe and rushed to her place.

"This is quite obviously a trap," I said, a minute into the ride.

"You're serious about this vampire shit?"

"Yeah. Wish I wasn't. You remember old man Skinner?"

Aaron chuckled. "Think so. Wasn't that the eighty-year-old who whacked you over the head with a pipe?"

"Bit over two years ago, yep. He didn't want me finding evidence on his son. Sometimes, I wonder if I'm still lying in a hospital bed having a coma dream about vampires. Bet Crystal is actually a new, cute nurse that tries to talk to me at night."

"If you're dreaming, so am I," said Aaron.

"If I'm dreaming, you wouldn't be real,

merely a product of my mind."

He glanced at me. "I haven't slept in about sixteen hours. My brain can't handle heady shit like that right now. Trust me. You are awake."

"Oh, yeah. I figured. A dream wouldn't have all those long parts where nothing happened, like days sitting at my office waiting for a client to show up. The slow bits would've felt like a few minutes in a dream."

He laughed. "I see you put some thought into this."

"I had to. Do you think the human mind is ill-equipped to cope with things of a supernatural nature, so we try to come up with excuses like dreaming? Or do you think that comes from living in a society that's turned a blind eye to the wondrous and the strange?"

Aaron mulled it over, not speaking until we got caught at a red light a few minutes later. "If things like vampires and magic exist, our brains can handle them because they'd be part of creation, too. Denial is a powerful thing in the human psyche."

"Says the guy who isn't ready to accept vampires are real."

"I'm not the sort of person who just believes stuff without seeing proof. That doesn't make for a good police investigator."

I chuckled. "Hope you brought a change of

underwear. If you spend much time around me today, you're definitely going to see proof of vampires."

"If these things had the sheriff under some sort of mind control, why would they take her?"

"Because she slipped free. Vampires have some ability to read minds, but they don't just know stuff out of the blue. It's likely they still think Justine and I are involved, or maybe they're aware we broke up and simply know what I'd do."

"Which is?"

"Exactly what we're doing now: walk straight into their trap. I'm honestly over my relationship with her, but I still can't let her die, or even get hurt because of me. The best thing we could do is find her before dark, take advantage of the daytime when the vamps are forced to sleep."

The light changed; Aaron stepped a little too hard on the gas, chirping the tires. "Does that mean you think they're going to kill her as soon as they wake up?"

"If their goal in abducting her is to bait me, it would be foolish of them to kill her. I'm more worried that they're going to turn her."

"I don't think they'd do that," said Aaron.

"You decided to believe me?"

He chuckled. "Not just yet, but I'm thinking

logically here—as logically as I can on such a wild topic. If their goal is to take control of the sheriff's department, what good would it do them to make Sheriff Waters unable to go outside during the day? She wouldn't be of any use to them. And following that train of thought, she especially wouldn't be any use to them dead."

The man made some good points, which gave me some hope. "Okay, that makes sense. This is potentially stupid, but the events of Wakefield Manor last night have given me a foolish amount of confidence."

"What happened last night?"

"Except for one kid, the entire Wakefield family were vampires. Now, their greatest enemy is a feather duster."

"What?" He blinked at me.

I smiled at him. "Meaning, they're all just ashes."

"Did you just confess to murdering the entire Wakefield family?"

"No. They'd all been dead for years. We cleaned up some inhuman creatures pretending to be the Wakefields. The family kept the youngest, a girl named Blair, basically captive, intending on turning her into a vampire the day she turned eighteen."

"Max, do you have any idea how crazy you

sound?"

"I've a fair notion. But after everything I've seen, it doesn't sound so crazy. Give it until tonight before you call me nuts."

He stayed quiet for the rest of the ride to Justine's home. She owned—or at least paid a mortgage on—a modest house in a fairly new development, a suburban area in the northwest part of Shadow Pines. The developer had a dark sense of humor, naming her street Dead Oaks Lane. All the cul-de-sacs and side streets around here had morbid-sounding names. Probably because the holding company that built all the homes wanted to capitalize on the 'tragedy tourism.' Who wouldn't want to live on Skeleton Crossing or Widow's Way?

Justine's blue Ford pickup still sat in her driveway. Aaron pulled up right behind it and cut the engine.

We got out of the police Tahoe and made our way to the front door.

"Whoever did this made entry via the back." Aaron pointed out the lack of damage here, then led me around through a gate to the backyard.

Her sliding glass patio door had been broken open, the latch plate hung from the doorjamb on one bent screw, the other one lost. The handle twisted to the right, the door under it warped.

"Yeah. Definitely vampires."

"How the heck are you so sure?"

I pointed at the mangled handle and ripped metal. "Someone with beyond human strength simply ripped it open, breaking the latch."

"Anyone could have done that with a sledgehammer."

"Possibly, but sledging this thing open would have scuffed, dented, or scratched the handle." I gestured at the grip, which was merely bent—no evidence of a sharp impact from a hard object.

Aaron leaned closer. "That's true, but still kind of a flimsy argument. Maybe they tied a rope to it and pulled with an ATV or something."

"No tire tracks ripping up the ground back here." I pointed behind me, then stepped into the kitchen. "Do you have any idea what time this happened?"

"Only that it would have been earlier than five a.m. That's when she gets up. If someone broke in after that, we'd be finding bullet holes in this door."

"Yeah. Her alarm is set for five. Even on weekends." I shuddered, remembering her strict schedule... and the occasional problems it caused in our relationship. "Seriously, waking up that early on a Saturday is a violation of the Geneva Accord."

Aaron didn't laugh, though his grim expression softened a little. "I didn't find much in the house except for signs of a fight in the bedroom."

Straight ahead, a doorway out of the kitchen opened to a dining room, then the living room. To the right, a hallway led to two bedrooms, a bathroom, and a couple closets. My gaze went straight to the pair of bullet gouges on the wall near the master bedroom. Blood spritz surrounded both holes.

I approached and examined the damage. The angle of entry to the drywall said the shots came from the bedroom, which led me to conclude Justine had been shooting defensively—as opposed to attackers returning fire *toward* her.

"She'd been awake, or at least woke up when they attacked. She's not a heavy sleeper."

Aaron nodded. "Yeah."

I headed into the bedroom. The air stank like a corpse had been stored there for a weekend. Aaron didn't react to the smell, which confirmed to me that it came from vampires. He couldn't detect it. More blood spray stained the walls by the door and also spattered on the louvered closets to my left. One bullet hole in the ceiling had blood around it, two more holes more directly above the bed had no blood. A scattering of empty 9mm shell casings littered the bed and rug. I counted eleven. Her department-issued Sig Sauer lay on the carpet in the corner beneath a gouge in the wall.

The bedding was half on the floor, as though her abductor threw it aside. Two dents in the drywall behind the headboard—that lined up with the posts—said one of them probably jumped on her. Justine and I had been, ah, somewhat energetic in the sack, but I've never rammed a headboard into a wall hard enough to dent it. Those marks were definitely recent.

"Breaking the door open probably woke her up with enough time to grab her weapon. She fired as soon as she saw someone in the hallway, kept firing as they entered the room and jumped on the bed." I pointed up. "One shot hit her attacker, the other two shots probably went off after they grabbed her arm and pushed the gun away. The attacker tore it out of her grip and threw the Sig aside." I pantomimed tossing the gun.

"Yeah. I pretty much figured that part out already. I'm stuck on the 'who' of it. What makes you think vampires did this?"

"I'm sure you're not going to accept that I can smell them here. So… consider that we've got two bullet holes in the hallway with blood spatter. Three on the wall by the door and one in the ceiling that also have blood spray. Justine put *seven* bullets into someone and the only blood anywhere in here is the spray from the shots. I dunno about you"—I faced Aaron —"but no normal person would be jumping on Justine's bed and overpowering her after taking seven bullets."

"Not without PCP involved," said Aaron.

"Also, don't you think there would be blood all over the place? There's hardly any. That tells me the person or people she shot had bodies that didn't like losing blood."

Aaron looked around at the floor. "They might've been grazing wounds. She'd have been firing in a completely dark room."

"*Seven* grazing wounds? That defies probability. Plus, a grazing wound deep enough for spray to hit the wall would've left dribbles on the rug or mattress. The *only* blood here is what the bullets carried to the walls. No drips, no bloody handprints, smears, or anything else."

"That doesn't even seem possible." Aaron set his hands on his hips.

"I doubt she loaded silver bullets, so the wounds would have stopped bleeding instantly."

"They heal *that* fast?" Aaron blinked.

"Nah. They just don't bleed unless they suffer a massive wound—like having their head cut off or guts ripped out by a werewolf. Clean-up is usually easy. Everything, even the blood stains, turns to ash. I'm guessing that this blood didn't ash over because the vampire it came from hasn't been destroyed."

"We shouldn't even be in here now, contaminating evidence."

"This isn't a case any crime lab is going to solve. She most likely unloaded on the first guy to enter the room, but I think we're looking at three or four vamps being here last night. Regardless of how many she hit, her bullets didn't slow them down."

Aaron paced, trying not to step on spent shell casings. "So, you have no idea where they took her?"

"Not yet. But they *did* take her. That means she's probably not dead yet."

He stopped walking around and stared at me. "What happened between you two?"

"You want the long or the short version?"

"Short."

"I was an asshole."

He blinked. "That's it?"

"Yeah, pretty much."

"How long is the long version?" Aaron chuckled.

"She kept pestering me to get a normal job instead of working for myself as a PI. I didn't want to get one. Cases had me out the door at all the wrong hours. Didn't spend enough time with her. Apparently, I also didn't truly listen to anything she said. Didn't respect her independent personality. Also, I considered a strong woman like Justine Waters fascinating while mostly crushing on her as an object of sexual attraction rather than treating her as a living, breathing person with actual wants and needs. The sex was amazing, but that's all we had. Our personalities meshed about as well as sweet pickle relish on pancakes with extra maple syrup. Last few weeks we were together, she kept dangling last chances. I still don't know if I really was that oblivious and didn't notice, or my subconscious knew we'd never work out and made the decision to stop me from saving the relationship."

Aaron blinked. "Dude…"

I sighed, hands on my hips. "Well, you did ask for the long version."

"I thought you two got along."

"We do… in a professional, co-worker sort of way. Just not romantically. We'd have gotten along even better if she hadn't been influenced by vampires. However, their mental control over her had nothing to do with us not working out. As far as I know, the vamps only influenced her to help them conceal the true nature of their activities. Mostly by passing off murders as 'animal attacks.' She might have done other things such as ignoring certain complaints or helping with permits, real estate, that sort of thing. Really, I don't know the full extent of it."

"That sounds bad. It would sound even worse if I really believed anything you said."

I laughed. "This town has a way of draining the skepticism out of anyone. Ever notice the look in people's eyes whenever they talk about the spooky stuff? It didn't occur to me until after I'd seen vampires in person and believed. Now, I can't help but feel that eight out of ten people here know about vampires but won't talk openly about them. I used to be a skeptic, too."

"What convinced you?"

"The wind."

"Come again?" Aaron raised an eyebrow.

I raised my hand a little and stirred a breeze inside the room. "The day I discovered I could control the wind, it didn't make any sense to remain a skeptic."

"Freaky. Are you really doing that?"

After a few minutes of me increasing the breeze and letting it fall off, Aaron realized the strength of the wind matched my hand motions. Considering most of the color drained from his cheeks, I figured he'd taken a step closer to believing I'm not a deranged serial killer.

Regardless of how much or little he believed me, it didn't bring us any closer to finding Justine. We had to do something... but the vampires could've taken her anywhere. My thoughts jumped to the boarding house where Piper and Derek had holed up, but I'd blasted the boards off the windows. The vamps would know that house no longer offered secrecy, but if they wanted me to go after Justine, that's exactly where they'd have brought her. Or, possibly, the Wakefield estate. That didn't seem likely for one big reason—Justine's abduction occurred simultaneously with our raid on the estate. If the abductors brought her there, we'd have seen them coming.

"I should probably enlist some help. A search from the air, maybe? Can you help with that?" I asked. "They might have taken her to Shadow Pines Manor, assuming that would be the first place I'd look. But going out there's a haul."

"We could split up, cover more ground that way. And I could help with the air search, sure. Usually, that needs Sheriff Waters to sign off on the helicopter, but since she's missing... Alvarez will go up without the paperwork."

Did I mention Shadow Pines has a crapton of money for such a little town? Where else would a police department overseeing a town of under a thousand people have its own helicopter?

I pulled out my phone. "And I know someone who could check the boarding house for us in a few seconds." My half-succubus girlfriend could teleport to places she'd already been. She didn't need weapons or clothes to merely scout the place. Being unarmed wouldn't matter since she could turn completely invisible. "Give me a sec."

Chapter Two
Witch Way to Go

Ringtone played in my ear three times before Crystal answered.

The din of a busy location in the background sounded like the local mall, Pines Court.

"Hey, babe," she said. "What's up?"

"I was going to ask you to check out the old boarding house if you could, you know, *pop* over there real quick. Justine's been abducted by our, umm, friends. Need to know if she's there. Not asking you to pull a one-woman commando raid. Just scout."

One nice thing about dating a woman who could see into my mind? She didn't have to doubt me when I told her I'd gotten over Justine and no longer had any romantic feelings for her. Succubi, even half ones, were creatures of emotion. She completely understood how I could still have a sense of protectiveness toward my ex. Even though the two of us never served together as cops or soldiers, we had that sort of ex-duty-partner relationship. Admittedly, the vampire stuff basically put us on opposite teams and strained our friendship to a point, but I couldn't let the fiends kill her.

"I'm at The Court with my mother and Blair getting her a new wardrobe. We're almost done. As soon as we take her back home, I could check that place out. Oh, hey, I got a better idea."

"Uh oh."

"Ha. Ha. Check Justine's bathroom wastebasket or brushes for a clump of hair. Mother might be able to help."

"I know I'm going to regret asking this, but what possible good can a clump of Justine's hair do us?"

Aaron tilted his head.

"I'll explain when you get here—I mean to the house, not the mall. We should be back home in about a half hour."

"Okay. Thanks."

"Love you."

"I love you, too, babe." I smiled, then let her

hang up first.

"That was quick." Aaron raised an eyebrow.

"What's quick?"

"Already seeing someone else?"

"Justine and I have been over for months. And I didn't exactly run around looking for a woman. After what happened with Justine, I'd pretty much convinced myself that I'd die a bachelor... then Crystal fell into my life."

"Oh, no. You're seeing that Bradbury girl?"

"What's wrong with that?"

He grimaced. "Just some rumors going around. Family exiled her to Ironside. That doesn't usually happen unless someone screws up big time."

"It's a complicated mess but not her fault. Short version: she fell on her proverbial sword to suppress a worse scandal."

"Oh, wow. Interesting."

I leaned into the bathroom and rummaged the wastebasket. "Justine's going to kill me if she finds out I rooted around in her trash."

"Why are you rooting around in her trash?"

"Looking for a clump of hair."

"I don't even want to know."

I laughed. "My feelings exactly. But... if it could help. Hey, look for a hairbrush."

"Are you serious?"

"Yep."

He shrugged and wandered around to search. A brush in a drawer had some hair in it, and I found another clump in the wastebasket.

Aaron grabbed a plastic baggie from the kitchen and we pooled our collected hairs in it.

"This has weird written all over it," said Aaron. "Are you going to tell me voodoo is real, too?"

"Not sure where she's going with this. However, it does kinda sound like we should prepare ourselves for things to get even stranger."

"Great…" He looked around. "Next, you're going to tell me not to report this or bring in a crime scene crew, or get the state police involved."

"Do you want to be stuck standing around here all day playing detective or use that time to find Justine before something happens to her? And you already left the scene once to come after me."

Aaron glared at me, but not in a hateful way as much as a 'damn you for being right' way. "All right, fine. But if this turns out to be a wild goose chase, you will regret it."

"Understood. No wild geese." I shook my head. "Strictly domesticated ones."

***

We had too much time to go straight to the Bradbury estate—we'd get there before Crystal, her mother, and Blair returned from the mall. To eat some time and because Aaron sorely needed it, we stopped for coffee on our way to the estate. Now properly caffeinated, Aaron pulled up to the call box outside the gate at 10:22 a.m.

"Can I help you?" asked the Bradbury's butler from the speaker.

"Pierce," I said, voice raised. "It's Max. Crystal's expecting us."

"Ahh, yes. Very good, Mr. Long."

A buzz came from the speaker, and the motorized gate slid out of our way. Pierce Hodge appeared at the front door, waiting patiently as we parked, got out, and walked across the courtyard to him. After a nod of greeting, he led us to a sitting room on the second floor. Crystal, barefoot in jeans and a pink sweater, sprang out of her chair and ran over to hug me. Little Blair, barefoot in jeans and a black cat T-shirt, sat on a sofa, nose buried in a Kindle. Sophia wore a long, plain dress. She watched us carefully.

"Hey, babe." Crystal kissed me, then leaned to the right to peer around me. "Who's that?"

"Deputy Aaron Wilson," he said, nodding.

"Given my past with Justine, I was at the top of his list of suspects." I winked.

Aaron held up the baggie of hair. "Can someone explain why you asked for this?"

"Sure." Crystal swiped the baggie from him and carried it over to her mother.

Sophia looked at me. "What's going on, Max?"

I took a deep breath. "Vampires abducted Justine. We don't know for sure what their reasons are yet, but my suspicion is that they're planning to use her to bait a trap for me. I asked Crystal to check the old boarding house, but she mentioned you could somehow find her with, um, hair."

"Maybe, we'll see." Sophia held up the baggie. "This is quite more than needed."

"How's it going, kid?" I asked, smiling at Blair.

She grinned. "Great! I didn't have a nightmare last night. I thought for sure I'd see half-eaten vampires chasing me around. That werewolf tore them into little bits."

Aaron stared at her.

"She appears to be doing well." Sophia brushed a hand over the girl's head, already fully invested in becoming her new mom. "There are some odd mystical energies in her, but I don't think they'll be a problem."

I tightened my jaw, fearing the worst. "What sort of monster is she?"

Blair stuck her tongue out at me.

"Not that sort of mystical energy. Blair's very much a normal person. However, she has been either involved in or exposed to some manner of ritual magic."

"I don't like the sound of that at all."

Blair bit her lip. "I don't remember them doing anything weird to me. Mom doesn't believe they intended to sacrifice me or anything."

Sophia's eyes reddened. Crystal looked perplexed for a few seconds before she squeezed me while making a face at the child like she'd seen a basket full of abandoned kittens.

Oh, the kid referred to *Sophia* as 'Mom.' She wasn't referring to the vampire we ashed.

It took Sophia a moment to swallow the lump in her throat and regain the ability to speak. "Correct. It's not too strong and doesn't appear to be affecting her in any way."

"I never even saw them do magic." Blair swished her feet side to side. "If they did something like that, I was too small to remember it. I haven't done anything strange other than living in a mansion with an army of vampires."

Sophia stood. "Pardon me for a few minutes.

I will return soon." She walked out of the room.

While we waited for her to come back, Aaron and I filled Crystal in on what we found at Justine's house. That conversation didn't take long, so she brought up their quick shopping trip. Blair gushed about getting new clothes for the first time in years, repeatedly thanking Crystal and going on about how happy she was to have a real home where no one locked her in her bedroom.

At talk of being locked in her room, Aaron started asking her questions. Her answers about multiple dangerous escapes involving climbing down the outside wall of the manor house progressively made his jaw hang open wider and wider. About the only decent thing her undead 'caretakers' had done was providing her with tutors. She had roughly a seventh-grade education despite being of age to be in fifth. Also, she desperately wanted to go to a normal school and have friends. To that end, she'd begged Sophia not to simply have her tutored at home.

Speaking of Sophia, Crystal's mother walked back in carrying a wooden tray with several small boxes and a shallow bowl. She set it on the coffee table, opened one of the boxes, and arranged five candles around the bowl.

We more or less stood there in curious

silence while she gathered pinches of dried roots, crumbled leaves, and some manner of grey powder from containers in the other boxes, adding each to the bowl atop a tiny disk of charcoal. Sophia lit the candles while muttering in a foreign language. I half wanted to call it Latin, but I didn't know for certain. Sounded like it.

Once the little charcoal nugget had turned completely grey, she took a pinch of Justine's hair and added it to the bowl on top of the burning ember. The hairs incinerated way too fast to be normal, bursting into a puff of smoke like old-timey flash powder. Sophia gathered the miniature cloud in her left hand, staring into it—with eyes that had gone completely white. Her strawberry blonde hair wavered as if in a breeze, though the air in the room hung perfectly still.

Aaron and I both leaned back, somehow managing not to yelp in surprise. Crystal didn't react at all.

Blair gasped and whispered, "Cool!"

Yeah, that kid's going to get into trouble someday.

After a moment, Sophia's blue irises reappeared. She gazed into space, dazed and out of it. Eventually, she blinked in a rapid flutter. "She is near to death, but has not been injured. I saw a great chasm. Grey stone. She is unable to move. The woman who belongs to this hair is not more than ten miles away."

"Only place I can think of that even remotely qualifies as a 'great chasm' within ten miles is the quarry." I squeezed my hands into fists.

"That's far enough out of town that no one would hear gunfire." Crystal gave me an 'I'm coming with you' look.

"What just happened here?" asked Aaron.

"She performed a divination," said Blair as casually as if she'd said 'she went to get water.'

I scratched my head. "Your mother is a wizard—or whatever you call it."

Crystal wagged her eyebrows. "Of course. Did you expect a normal woman to have a daughter like me?" She flashed a cheesy smile at Blair. "Sorry, the family's a little weirder than I let on before."

"That's not weird. That's *awesome*." Blair gestured at the tray of 'magic stuff.' "Normal is boring. But… it might not be the greatest idea in the world to summon demons."

Sophia put an arm around her. "I didn't summon a demon. Crystal's father is a fey trickster. And his services required a certain price that…" She squeezed Crystal's hand. "I have absolutely no regrets over."

"Wait, you didn't summon him specifically because you wanted me?" Crystal feigned insult.

"If I'd have known you'd be the result, I absolutely would have. But, no… do you recall approximately twenty-six years ago when Graham Farrington had a particularly nasty streak of rotten luck?"

"I would've been two years old, so no." I chuckled.

"Can't say I remember much from when I was four." Aaron shook his head.

"Likewise," added Crystal. "Considering I'd have been an egg at that point."

"I wasn't even alive then." Blair made a silly face.

Sophia smiled. "Well, Graham adored meddling around with mysticism. The Farringtons always did have a habit of teasing powers better left alone. I'd had something of a prophetic dream that he'd cause quite a bit of pain and suffering in town, so I did what I could to frustrate his goals without killing him. For several months, he experienced incredibly bad luck. Numerous business ventures began to fail, he couldn't go near a flight of stairs without ending up in a cast, and he became dreadfully terrified of motor vehicles. Forget flying. The last I heard of him, he'd gone to South America, vowing never to return to this 'cursed' town."

"Wow." Blair blinked. "Something like that's going to have nasty karmic blowback, even if you didn't kill him."

Sophia sighed, head bowed. "It's possible that's why Dana died. Or Sterling. Maybe both. Sometimes, I wonder if he gave me Crystal because he knew what would happen to Dana." Dana was, of course, Crystal's sister who'd recently been killed by a 'big cat' aka vampire.

"*Pshaw.*" Crystal hugged her mother. "You know that's not true. Having to put up with younger me was the karmic blowback."

Her mother laughed.

"Sorry to ruin the moment, but you did say Justine's 'near death.' We should get out there right away." I reflexively grabbed under my left arm where my .44 revolver wasn't. I'd left it back at my office since pulling that cannon out of a drawer in front of an upset deputy wouldn't have ended well for me. Going to the quarry without it felt like getting into a fight naked, but if Crystal could take on vampires while literally naked, I could handle not having a gun on me. Besides, I had the elements… and bullets didn't do much to the undead other than piss them off and ruin their wardrobe.

Aaron gestured at her. "Let's assume that anything going on right now is real. How can she possibly be near death but not injured? Isn't that a contradiction?"

"Not at all." Sophia flashed a knowing smile. "If someone had a gun to your head, a tiny motion of their finger is all it would take to kill you. In that situation, you would be close to death but not hurt."

Blair made a 'duh' face at him, but kept her mouth shut. Smart kid.

"Oh. Right." Aaron rubbed his hand down his face. "This woo woo stuff is making my brain shut off, plus I'm coasting on little sleep."

"Grabbing shoes," said Crystal while running for the door.

"Why bother?" Sophia smiled. "You're going to end up bare butt again, anyway."

"Mother!" fumed Crystal, then froze. "Are you being sarcastic or prophetic?"

"Realistic. You know when you were small, we couldn't keep you dressed."

"That wasn't my fault. For a while, every time I sneezed, I'd teleport across the room."

Sophia flashed an impish smile. "And you didn't exactly run right back over to put them on."

"First world problems," deadpanned Blair.

"More like first dimension problems. I'll be right back." Crystal ran off.

"Why are we bringing a civilian with us?"

asked Aaron.

"Don't you mean a *second* civilian? Last time I checked, I didn't have a badge. And she's far from a normal civilian." I patted him on the shoulder. "I'd say trust me, but you're probably getting sick of hearing that. We're bringing her because we are doing everything possible to make sure Justine stays alive."

Aaron exhaled. "All right. Good enough for me."

"Can I go, too?" asked Blair.

"No!" said everyone at once—including Crystal shouting from down the hallway.

"Just kidding." Blair laughed, then pointed at me. "But that face you made."

Chapter Three
The Quarry

I let Crystal have the front seat and climbed into the back. The Sheriff's Department Tahoe didn't have a prisoner cage, so despite being in the rear seat of a police vehicle, I didn't feel awkward.

Aaron drove in quiet without me having to tell him to. He'd put the bar lights on to get through downtown, but once we hit the outskirts, he shut off the flashers and forced himself to drive at an inconspicuously normal pace.

"What's your read on the kid?" I asked.

"You talking to me or Crystal?" Aaron made momentary eye contact via the rear-view mirror.

"Mostly her." I patted the back of her seat.

Crystal shifted around to look at me. "How do you mean?"

"Feels strange to me that she's so at ease with her whole family being wiped out. That kid's what, ten? She claims to have been basically held prisoner her entire life, then she witnesses the last minute or so of us destroying vampires who used to be her family—and she is unfazed. Doesn't that seem a little odd?"

"She's tough. And she's not unfazed, merely hiding it well. The girl's terrified and lonely. I'm sure once she feels secure in her new home, she's going to have something of a meltdown. At the moment, she still has her defenses up."

Aaron glanced at Crystal. "What are you, some kind of child psychologist?"

"I suppose." She examined her fingernails. "I've always had a knack for feeling out others' emotions."

"Oh, yeah? What am I feeling right now?

"Mostly exhausted, but also like your entire world's been turned upside down. You're worried about more than Justine. Feeling isolated, since most of the sheriff's department is gone. Am I right?"

"Holy shit," muttered Aaron.

"I take that as a yes."

"She's good." I grinned.

Aaron grabbed the mic from the dash. "Patty, this is 105, come back?"

"Go ahead, Aaron," said a voice from the radio, likely the dispatcher.

"Has anyone else showed up yet or are they all still missing?"

"A few, yes. It does feel kinda light. Think the sheriff screwed up and approved too many people on the same day to take vacation. I don't see or hear anyone now, but a few deputies are —or were here earlier. Not long enough for me to tell who, though. They went right back out. Any word on Sheriff Waters?"

Aaron furrowed his brows. "Not yet. Still looking."

"I haven't been able to get a hold of her either," said Patty. "The mayor's been by to talk to her. Not sure how much longer he's going to wait. It's not like her to vanish."

"Unconfirmed at this time, but I suspect disappearing wasn't her idea."

"What do you mean 'not her idea?'" asked Patty.

"Still investigating. I'll let you know as soon as I find something." Aaron let off the mic and muttered, "Son of a bitch."

"What?" I asked.

"He's just frustrated, Max," said Crystal,

answering for him. "Probably because he thinks we're wasting time chasing witchcraft."

"Something like that," grumbled Aaron. "And no one likes a know-it-all."

Crystal leaned closer to him. "Oh, wow. You really are in need of sleep. Kinda on the grumpy side."

"Yeah. Been up since yesterday. Caught a few Zs on the plane. Was gonna ask Sheriff Waters if I could take the day to recover, but she hadn't come in yet. Now I'm running around like a headless chicken. The only reason I'm even taking this ride is Max made freakin' fire appear in his hand. So help me... if it's a trick."

Simultaneously, Crystal and I said, "It's not."

"So you're sure Blair is normal?" I asked Crystal after a few moments of silence.

"Yep. Well, as normal as a kid could be living around vampires. Mother thinks she's absorbed a lot of supernatural energy, but we're not sure what if any effect that could have on her. According to Grandmother, the other families are all blowing up with gossip about what happened to erase all the Wakefields but one—and most of them didn't even realize Blair existed. A few are even claiming she's not really part of the family line. But, even Grandmother said she's the spitting image of Madeline."

I cocked an eyebrow. "The one we saw pulling the blood out of the fridge?"

"Yeah."

"That woman didn't look old enough to have a ten-year-old daughter… unless she got pregnant as a teen."

Crystal smirked at me. "Max, we're dealing with vampires. She probably had the kid and two years later got turned. She froze at twenty-whatever."

"Right." I groaned, rubbing my forehead. "Guess Aaron's not the only one here who needs a good long sleep."

"Anyway, I think Blair came to terms with her family being gone a long time ago. She didn't think of the vampires with any sense of familial love at all. To her, they were monsters dressed up in the faces of people she once knew. She's felt totally alone for most of her life and it's going to take her some time to accept she isn't anymore. Already, she's attached herself to Mother. The girl is *starved* for affection and my mother is all too ready to give it to her."

"She's already referring to Sophia as Mom."

"Exactly." Crystal stared up at the roof. "Mother cried so damn hard the first time Blair called her that. Okay, correction, she cried when I whispered that the girl was sincere and not just saying that to manipulate her."

"Either we're not in Kansas anymore or everyone in this damn town is nuts," muttered Aaron.

"I haven't even mentioned the UFOs," I said.

Aaron slowly turned his head to stare at me. "You have got to be kidding."

"Yeah, sorry." I chuckled. "At least if UFOs exist, I haven't seen one."

"Thank the good lord... though, admittedly, aliens seem a little easier to wrap my head around."

I grinned and shifted my gaze back to Crystal. "What do you think about the magic stuff your mother mentioned with her? Some kind of energy?"

"Umm. I'm not really sure. Mother couldn't sniff out the exact nature of it, so it can't be too significant. Like she said, it is most likely residual energy from spending so much time surrounded by paranormal beings. Or just that house. I've never been in a place that frightened me like that. That mansion has some serious dark aura stuff going on."

"Yeah. I know what you mean. It unsettled me, too."

"You two are starting to freak me out. It sounds like you really believe this stuff." Aaron slowed down as we neared the area of the quarry. He'd taken us in via the road most people considered the 'back' way, since it looped around the opposite side of the quarry from town. That offered higher ground and less chance of being spotted.

"We do." I leaned into the front seat, pointing at a boulder the size of a moving van. "Park behind that rock. We get any closer with this truck, they're going to see us."

"They? But it's the middle of the day." Despite his protest, Aaron parked behind the giant rock.

"Vampires can have human thralls," I said. "I sincerely doubt they've left her somewhere completely alone. Even if they did, no sense being reckless when Justine's life is at risk."

"Agreed. Fine." Aaron cut the engine. "Thralls?"

"Mind-controlled slaves."

He stared straight up at the Tahoe's roof. "Good God."

We got out and eased the doors closed to avoid making noise. Aaron grabbed a pair of binoculars from the back. We moved around the boulder and crawled up to the quarry edge flat on our chests.

While Aaron looked around with the binoculars, I did the best I could with my eyes alone. The wall below us had a steep angle that went about thirty feet down to a dirt road carved out of the cliff that ran approximately a quarter mile to the left before reaching the quarry bottom behind a cluster of abandoned dump trucks. An old crane a fair distance off from there had its boom extended way up with some manner of square metal box dangling from the cable. A handful of men wandered about. Though I couldn't make out their faces from here, they obviously carried rifles. Two sedans and a pickup sat in a cluster even farther away than the crane.

"Got her," whispered Aaron. "Crane."

He handed me the binoculars.

I zoomed in on the area of the crane. A man in workers' clothes sat in the cab at the controls, though he appeared to be absorbed in the contents of his cell phone screen. Another man leaned against the crane outside, holding an AK-47 sideways. He, too, wore a flannel shirt and jeans but had a posture more befitting of a soldier pulling sentry duty. Of course, he didn't have the physique of a soldier unless the Army added an infantry specialization for beer consumption.

"I don't see her," I whispered.

"Look up. She's in the… cage."

"The hell?"

I panned my view up the crane boom to the metal box. It had to be the cab of a mine elevator, basically a steel mesh box. 'Cage' was a good word for it considering a chain and padlock held the door shut. Justine lay inside wearing an oversized T-shirt 'nightgown' as well as handcuffs. Someone had tied her ankles together with a black cord. I guessed they'd covered her mouth with tape since she a constant stream of threats and curses didn't echo over the quarry. At a guess, she dangled maybe ninety feet off the ground. After a minute or three of looking at her, she began squirming, giving me a brief glimpse of her face. She did have silver duct tape over her mouth and the mother of all scowls. I'd made Justine plenty pissed off, but she never glared at me like *that*. Pretty sure that glare said she would legit kill someone and worry about the paperwork later.

"What the heck is the point of this?" I muttered.

"If you're right about vampires, your notion of this being a trap for you makes sense. Check out the linkage holding the cage to the crane cable."

I zoomed in on that spot. A yellow-painted

boxy mechanism connected the hook to the cable. "Some kind of pulley?"

"That's a breakaway link. Crane operator has a button that will drop it. Your mother was right, Crystal. Sheriff Waters *is* an inch from death. The bastard hits that button, she's gonna drop nine stories."

"Probably intending on using that to make me surrender myself." I scowled, then looked around at the men. "I'm counting six guys, all armed with rifles."

"Yeah. Saw that. They don't seem like they're out of it or anything." Aaron exhaled hard out his nostrils. "I can't believe I'm going to ask this, but can you tell if they're being, you know, mind-controlled or doing this of their own free will?"

"Pretty much impossible to know that without being a vampire or a telepath," I muttered.

"I might be able to tell if I get closer." Crystal reached for the binoculars, so I let her have a look. "Oh, wait, never mind. They're definitely thralls."

"How do you know?" I asked. "Not doubting you, merely curious what gave it away."

"They have bored expressions."

"Uhh," said Aaron. "They're standing around a quarry doing nothing."

"And guarding the kidnapped head of the

Shadow Pines police department. None of them seem anxious, worried, or much of anything. Like robots set to task." She handed me back the binoculars.

I frowned. "The two guys at the crane are the biggest problem. Aaron, you got a rifle in the Tahoe?"

"No, just a shotgun. Not going to outrange those guys. If they see us coming, they're going to drop her. Shit. If you're right about vampires, we need to figure something out before it gets dark. State police or National Guard won't get here in time to make a difference."

"Dammit." I didn't want to say it, but I worried ten times more about charging in down there than I did about taking on all the vampires in Wakefield Manor. To be fair, if those vampires had all carried combat rifles, I'd have been equally concerned last night. Still, no reason to panic as we had a decent amount of daylight left before the vampires woke up. "Does the sheriff's department have sniper rifles?"

"Give me a few minutes," said Crystal. "I got it."

Aaron looked over at her, clearly doubting what she could possibly do here. "Sit tight, Crystal. They can kill the sheriff with one button as soon as they see us."

"Exactly." Crystal disappeared, or at least

her body did. An apparently empty sweater and jeans hovered beside me. "You said *see* us coming."

"What the…" Aaron blinked. "Oh, damn. I really am hallucinating. Is she..."

I grinned. "Invisible. Yes."

Crystal's sweater bunched up as she removed it. A red lace bra floated in space over her jeans. "Guess Mother was being prophetic after all." The rest of her clothes peeled away from the invisible body under them and fell to the ground. "Bare ass again."

Chapter Four
This is Careful

Poor Aaron gawked, dumbfounded as invisible Crystal took her jeans, sneakers, and socks off.

"What's the plan?" I asked.

"I'm going to slip down there and take care of the two guys at the crane. As soon as there's no one in reach of the kill button, you guys can charge in or do whatever you're going to do."

"Can you maybe fly up to Justine, poke a finger through the mesh to touch her and teleport her out of there?"

"Teleport?" stammered Aaron.

"No. While I *can* bring someone with me, I basically have to be carrying them for it to work. If they're in contact with the ground, only I vanish."

I nodded at where her voice came from. "Okay. Take care of those two and we'll start running as soon as you do so."

"Going now," said Crystal.

A trail of bare footprints formed in the dusty ground away from us to the edge of the cliff. A leathery *fwoof* noise came from a few feet past the edge seconds later. I guessed she jumped onto her wings.

"Man, I am absolutely not equipped to deal with this crap. Did your girlfriend just strip down naked and leap into the quarry?" Aaron chuckled. His chuckle sounded slightly... hysterical.

"Yes. And keep it together, man."

"Trying."

"Good. And to be clear... she turned invisible first, then stripped, then jumped to fly into the quarry."

"Fly? Not teleport? And did I just say those words?"

"You did. And yes, she's got wings."

Aaron nodded, looking a little queasy. "She didn't have wings."

"She does, but she can put them away somehow. They come out when she needs them."

The poor deputy stared at me with a look like he was about to go home and drink an entire bottle of something strong.

I smiled at him. "This is where you say something like 'they aren't paying me enough for this shit.'"

He grinned... or tried to. "They aren't. Be right back. Grabbing the shotgun."

"Okay." I nodded, then resumed watching the crane via the binoculars.

As Aaron crawled off, I noted that Justine appeared to be trying to attack the cord binding her ankles. If not for the duct tape over her mouth, she would've set a world record for the most profanity spewed in a single hour, of that I had no doubt. Her captors hadn't cared at all for her comfort. Luring me into a trap was the only reason I could think of for them to dangle her up there like literal bait on a giant fishing pole. The crane held her so far off the ground she hovered almost four stories higher than the ground level surrounding the quarry pit. Anyone driving by could see the box on the cable, but probably wouldn't notice someone was in it, much less a tied up, extremely pissed off sheriff.

"Patty, it's Aaron, do you copy? Need backup," said Aaron from near the truck.

Shit. I rolled over on my side and flailed an

arm at him, trying to wave him off.

"Patty?" He gave me a weird look. When I kept waving at him like he stood inside a burning house, he let go of the mic and crept back over carrying his shotgun.

"Don't send out a radio call. Your dispatcher said people didn't come in today, anyway, remember?"

"Yeah… so? Someone's gotta be available."

"So, if the vampires have done to the deputies who didn't show up for work today what they did to those men down there, they'll hear you broadcasting over the radio that we're at the quarry. Guarantee one of them's going to make a cell phone call and whatever advantage of surprise we have is going to be lost."

"Dammit." Aaron flopped on the ground, swiped the binoculars, and belly crawled to the edge, looking back and forth. "Whew."

"Whew, what?"

"None of the guys down there are deputies." He handed me the binoculars back. "Keep an eye on that crane and let me know when we can move. And, dammit."

"Now what?"

Aaron gestured toward the edge of the quarry. "We're gonna be wide open sitting ducks."

"Nah. I got that handled. Mostly."

He quirked an eyebrow at me.

I zoomed in on the crane again. Still, nothing happening. Maybe Crystal had to land far enough off that they didn't hear her wings fluttering. Or she could be looking around for any surprises. Yeah, that sounded more like her. She's methodical. Well, somewhat methodical. If a person could be simultaneously methodical and impulsive, that would be Crystal.

"No one answered," said Aaron. "Patty didn't respond to me. That should've at least caused one or two deputies to start chiming in for status checks."

"Good chance the vamps went after more than Justine last night. Be glad they didn't target you."

"I was on a plane remember? Didn't land until almost five this morning due to delays. I haven't slept yet. Man, ain't this some bullshit. Having to go back to work the next morning right after seven days in Florida."

"Pretty sure Justine's having a worse day. You might be all that's left of the police around here, bub. Well… you and Justine."

"Be straight with me, Max. What the hell is going on here?"

"Already told you. Vampires."

He sighed. "I still think that's bullshit."

"I wish it was. If you're not careful, when

the sun goes down tonight, you're going to end up either drinking blood or drinking shitloads of whisky."

Aaron muffled a laugh. "Drunk retired cop is such a cliché."

"So is a PI with a bottle of Jack in his desk drawer—and I've got a bottle of Jack in my desk."

"That fits. We already did the 'they ain't paying me enough for this shit' thing with me. Surprised you haven't said something similar."

I chuckled. "I can't say that. No one is paying me at all for this job."

"This ain't a job." His good mood faded.

"No, not Justine. I mean getting rid of the vampires. *This* is helping a friend. Cleaning up Shadow Pines is the unpaid work."

"Oh." He swiped a hand over his sweaty face. "What's going on down there now?"

"Nothing yet. Crystal is probably snooping around to make sure we don't run into any unpleasant surprises."

"Man, your girl's got some nerve to go down there with nothing on."

"She's wearing invisibility. No one can see her. Invisibility works the same as clothes do, right?"

"Huh. Now that you mention it, yeah. I guess."

The crane door opened.

"Hang on. We're hot."

"What happened?"

"Crane door moved. Guy inside is looking confused… and just closed it again. She opened it. And he closed it again."

"Is she pranking him? The hell?"

This time, the crane door swung open all the way. Annoyed, the man inside leaned out to reach for it—and the door slammed right on his head.

"Operator's out cold. She walloped him in the head with the door. Other one's coming around to check on him. Second one is searching…" The guy walked around the back end of the crane, circling it. An AK-47 floated out of the operator's compartment and glided after him. The crane blocked my view, but shadows on the ground showed the floating rifle swing up and bean the guy over the head, knocking him into a stagger.

He fired a shot into the ground.

"Shit." I tossed the binoculars aside and leapt to my feet, raising my hands.

At my behest, strong winds whipped up around me, blanketing the area around us in a thick haze of dust. I didn't need to prompt Aaron. As soon as visibility dropped to about twenty feet, he sprang upright and tried to run down the steep hill. I fast-walked, moving as rapidly as I could while still concentrating on keeping the air and dust moving.

Gunfire popped from multiple locations ahead of us. I couldn't see a damn thing, but at least had the reassurance of no bullets whistling anywhere near me. The men down in the quarry probably wouldn't associate a spontaneous dust storm with me, but at this point, we couldn't take anything for granted.

The hill turned out to be a lot steeper than I expected. Redirecting the gale to blow uphill supported the two of us enough that we didn't lose our balance and go tumbling to a broken neck. I speed shimmied down the sharp incline, the dirt frequently crumbling out from under my feet. A near fall cost me my concentration on the wind, and losing that support—which I'd been leaning against—turned my nearly falling into actually falling.

Fortunately, I'd made it reasonably close to the road at that point and only tumbled over twice before skidding to a stop on flat ground. I sat up to find Aaron sprinting down the quarry road toward the cluster of dump trucks.

Wow. A legit hero, that one.

Clanks came from high overhead in time with the gunshots. Shit! They're shooting at Justine. I called a crosswind to clear the dust haze. Four men stood out in the open, taking pot shots up at the dangling mine elevator. At a guess, I estimated my range to them at about 300 yards. A doable shot if I had a rifle, but lightning? Maybe. But not so much with fire. Projecting flames from my hands petered out at like twenty-five feet or so. No way could I reach them with fire.

I focused on one guy randomly, aimed both my arms at him, and called out with every bit of desire possible that lightning stop the son of a bitch from hurting Justine. A bolt of electricity shot up from my fingertips and exploded into a distant hillside. Oops. Ignoring that, I continued to concentrate on him.

Two seconds later, a second shaft of normal lightning fell from the cloudless sky and nailed the dude in the head. A *boom* as loud as a naval cannon accompanied a concussive wave that knocked the other shooters off their feet. The jagged arc of electricity racing down the man's body into the ground burned itself into my retinas. Smoking, he careened over like a man-nequin.

Okay, that's new. Every time I've invoked lightning before it shot from my hands. I must be angrier or more worried than I've admitted to myself.

Roaring like some kind of WWE wrestler,

Aaron charged the gunmen. I ran to my left, following the road since, unlike Crystal, a thirty-foot vertical drop would seriously screw up my plans for the rest of the day.

Amid a rumble of diesel, the crane started. Seconds later, the dangling mine elevator began to creep downward. No one appeared to be at the controls. Hopefully, Crystal huddled down, taking cover behind the console. It didn't make much sense for those idiots to shoot at an apparently empty seat, but dumber things have happened.

The stunned men knocked over by the lightning strike scrambled to get back to their feet. As soon as they tried to aim their rifles at Aaron, he opened fire with his shotgun, having closed to within range enough he could use it. Still too far away for fire or directing lightning from my fingertips, I focused elemental earth energy into the ground below the human thralls, causing the dirt to buckle, fouling their aim.

In seconds, Aaron had mowed them down.

I bee-lined for the crane. It had been a damn long time since I ran track in school. Okay, ten years isn't *that* long to some people, but it's long to me. Hiking is one thing; running is another. The mine elevator landed before I got to it. The crane door flew open. Bare footprints appeared in a rapid trail over to the 'cage.' The padlock popped open for no apparent reason and the chain went flying off to the side.

"Max!" shouted Crystal from right in front of me. "She's hit!"

Justine lifted her head, gawking at the door. "Mmt mmm mmk?"

I reached the cage door the same instant the tape peeled itself off Justine's face.

"It's okay. Don't panic," said invisible-Crystal.

"Max, what the fuck is going on?" rasped Justine.

I leapt in and crouched beside her, staring at a bloody wound in her right lower abdomen. Other than a copious amount of sweat on her face, and the veins standing out in her forehead, she didn't show much outward sign of pain. Yeah, that's Justine all right. The human version of an M1 Abrams tank.

"They got me," said Justine. "Not talking about the bullet. Why the hell did you have to upset the balance? You should've left them alone."

"You're blaming *him*?" shouted Crystal. "Seriously?"

Justine looked around. "Please tell me you hear that voice and I'm not going nuts."

"That's Crystal. And I'm trying to put things back to normal. Remember normal? Yeah, no one else does either, which is why the vamps have to go. The undead are going to stir shit as long as they're here. Doing what they want is the exact wrong way to handle this. You can't trust them. Trying to keep your head down and hope they leave you alone is no different from a cow standing around waiting to be slaughtered."

She let her head fall against the ground. "Bastards dragged me right out of bed."

Aaron jogged up to the door in the cage. "Crap! Sheriff!" He grabbed his shoulder mic. "Patty! I need an ambulance out to the old quarry STAT. Officer down!"

No response came.

He repeated the call.

Still nothing.

"That's not good," rasped Justine.

"Crystal, can you take her to the hospital?" I asked. "And by take her to the hospital, I mean teleport her ass there?"

"On it, Hang on, this might hurt a little."

Justine's body moved as invisible arms scooped her up. "Max, you got me shot."

I kept holding pressure on the wound. "Better shot than killed. None of us are safe in this town anymore. It's us or them, and I really want it to be them."

Justine groaned. "Whatever. Just get me to the goddamned hospital before I bleed out."

"Max," said Crystal. "Please grab my clothes on your way out. I'll meet you back at your office."

"You got it."

"What are you doing?" barked Aaron. "We need to get her to the hospital."

Justine disappeared, leaving a giant bloody T-shirt draped over my hand. A pair of cuffs and a tangle of black cord hit the ground.

"What the fuck?" Aaron gawked.

I dropped the shirt. Pretty sure she wouldn't want that one back. "Crystal just teleported Justine to the hospital. Right about now, she's probably working her charms on some orderly or nurse to make them not notice Justine appearing out of thin air."

"Are you serious?"

"No, I'm Max Long."

"I'm legit about to punch you right in the nose." Aaron stared at me.

I chuckled. "Justine's safe. Needed a tension breaker."

"What the hell are we supposed to do now?"

"You could call in the crime scene, but there appears to be a problem with your radio. That or the sheriff's department is empty."

He frowned.

I said, "Let's confiscate the weapons and get back to my office to meet Crystal. Justine's going to be in surgery for a while and then probably unconscious for the rest of the day. We have more immediate worries to deal with."

He nodded. "Let me guess. Vampires."

I patted him on the arm, smiling. "See, you're catching on."

Aaron shook his head. "Lord help me."

Chapter Five
Overrun

Aaron's willingness to gather up the kidnapper's weapons and leave the area surprised me.

I figured he'd want to secure the scene, bring in the coroner, maybe the state police. You know, do a proper investigation. Then again, as the old saying went, 'when you see someone teleport, your view of the world changes.' Okay, I made that one up. But nope. The deputy kept silent the whole time, although he did insist on taking cell phone pictures of the two cars and the pickup truck in case they 'mysteriously vanished' before a proper investigation could occur.

The odds of that happening—a real investigation—into what happened here were slim to nonexistent. Even without being mind-controlled, Justine would not file a report claiming that these men suffered mental domination from vampires and abducted her. In fact, I'd bet a good pile of cash that, officially, she would report that an 'unknown assailant' took a pot shot at her from the shadows. Maybe even a drunk hunter hitting her by accident.

Thankfully, it appeared as though the bullet struck her after bouncing off the metal grid of the mine elevator. I'd never claim to be a doctor or even a weapons expert, but her wound did look quite small for an AK-47 bullet. Justine appeared coherent enough to understand what happened to her, so maybe she'll tell the doctor she caught a ricochet after a near miss.

Either way, she'd be fine. At least, unless the vamps tried to go after her again in the hospital. I had two reasons to entertain the hope that wouldn't happen. One: I planned to go full on Rambo tonight and burn out as many undead as I could find. Two: they'd hopefully realize that we found her once and would do so again… so she made for *bad* bait.

The walk up the quarry road carrying four AK-47s sucked. I never thought of rifles as being all that heavy—until I had to carry four of them at once. Couldn't complain out loud though. Aaron carried another four plus three handguns. The manpower here might have been thralls, but they damn sure had come ready for a full on war.

Aaron secured all the guns in the back of the Tahoe, got in, and started the engine.

He really looked like he needed a nap. Or three.

"You want me to drive?" I asked.

Aaron stared at the boulder in front of us for a moment. "I could get reprimanded for allowing a civilian to operate a department vehicle. However, I could also get reprimanded for driving when I'm this tired. Screw it. We're already using the policy manual for toilet paper today."

We traded places.

Almost the instant the passenger door closed, Aaron fell asleep. I'd never really fantasized about being a cop of any kind, but driving an official vehicle *was* cool. I did resist the temptation to turn the lights on. Fate may not have given me movie star good looks, a giant brain, or enough athleticism to play professional sports, but I did have a lot of willpower. Or, as Justine would've put it, stubborn as hell.

Funny how almost anything good could be flipped around to sound negative.

Oh well.

It took twenty-two minutes to drive from the quarry back into Shadow Pines. I parked the Tahoe by my office, hopped out, and ran across the street to grab three burgers with cheese fries. A war with vampires couldn't be fought on an empty stomach after all.

That done, I headed back to the truck, grabbed Crystal's clothes, and went into the office. Yeah, I left Aaron to sleep it off. Little did he know, he was going to wake right back up into it.

"Are you here?" I called out.

"Yes," said Crystal from nowhere. "Oh, that smells good."

I set one bag and her clothes on her desk next to her keyboard, the other two on mine. Her clothing floated into the air, seemingly putting itself on an invisible body. She gave me a quick peek of her boobs by appearing a split second before the sweater covered her.

Mean girl, mean. Putting me in the mood for something we have no time to do.

"What did you do with the deputy?" asked Crystal.

"He's in the truck, sleeping. Poor guy."

While we ate, we filled each other in on what happened after she teleported out. My story was a lot more boring: carrying crap up a long hill to the truck. She'd been to the local hospital a few times, but didn't remember it all that well, so she'd teleported to the spot where ambulances usually pulled up to drop off critical patients. Her magic—as no other word really fit—didn't have any flashiness to it. No lights, no weird noises, she merely appeared out of thin air. They got lucky. No one noticed where Justine came from. That said, she's going to have a harder time explaining how she took a bullet and ended up at the hospital with no clothing then dealing with the mess at the quarry in a way that wouldn't get anyone sent to a mental institution.

"I shadowed her long enough to fog the minds of the medical staff. Everyone thinks they cut her clothing off in prep for surgery, but no one remembers where they put anything."

"Oh. Wow, you're handy." I grinned and took a bite of my burger.

"You have no idea." She ate a French fry in a way that I found *highly* distracting.

"But I am happy to report that Justine should be fine," said Crystal.

I let out the mother of relieved sighs. "Thank God."

"Freaked a couple doctors out when I left the operating room, but the door moving by itself didn't cause too much of a scene."

As I chuckled at the image, Aaron stumbled in, doing a spot-on impression of a zombie. He even made the incoherent moan sound perfect.

"Got you some lunch." I point at the third bag.

He grunted again, shambled over, and plopped down in one of the chairs facing my desk. It took him a few seconds to figure out how to open the bag. After giving me a thumbs-up, he proceeded to attack his food.

"I'm pretty sure things are seriously about to hit the fan," I said. "We need to find the vampires and take out as many as possible before dark."

Crystal wagged her burger at me while chewing. "Nice thought, but you know they aren't all going to be in one place, right?"

"A guy could hope."

She shook her head. "Each group or individual vampire has his or her own agenda. Remember, Piper and Derek lived with only a handful of their buddies at the Shadow Pines Manor. Meanwhile, the Wakefield vampires couldn't care less about Derek and Piper. Heck, there are vampires working for most of the Founding Families and sometimes that gets them into fights against each other."

"So if I understand what you're saying, we're going to be at this for a while… hunting them down."

She nodded, then took a bite.

I took in some air and snapped a small flame to life, letting it dance over my open palm. "There's gotta be something. Some key. Shadow Pines wasn't always so overrun. Sure, weird stuff happened around here ever since I was a little kid, but these past two or three years have been off the chart. You know, the energy in the air at the Wakefield place... I have half a mind to say that's the origin."

Crystal shrugged. "Maybe. But we already cleared it out. Consider this: the Farrington and Blackwood families have a lot of connections to vampires. Rumors claim a handful of each family became vampires. The Anworths won't even talk to vampires. That's part of the reason they had issues with the Bradburys. My in-laws don't trust vampires, but they do find them occasionally useful."

"Like when Darth Grandmother sent them after Nigel." I bit off a quarter of my burger in one chomp.

"Exactly. Think of it like nukes. The Bradburys only used them because everyone else did. Now, the Darceys also don't trust them. We *know* what they are."

"Your mother's maiden name."

"Right. I'm more Darcy than Bradbury even

though I legally have my not-real-father's name."

"Considering your mother appears to be a bit of a witch—and I mean that in the nicest way possible—it doesn't surprise me her kin are wary of vampires."

Crystal gazed off into the distance, lost in thought. "Pretty sure the Musgraves and Omonds have the occasional contact with vamps, but I can't say for sure if they're as dependent on them as the Bradburys, Blackwoods, Farringtons, and Wakefields. Though, the Wakefields aren't an issue anymore."

"I sincerely hope no other family is as into vampirism as they were. Not sure how well we'd do trying to take on another entire manor house full of undead without some werewolf backup."

Aaron gawked at me. "Freakin' werewolves?"

"Yep. Don't worry though. They're usually not a problem."

"They've been victimized by bad PR," added Crystal.

"So, Farrington and Blackwood are next in line." I stuffed my face with fries. "Sounds like a good place to start."

Aaron waved at me in a 'hang on a sec' way while he finished chewing. "Wait. We can't just go kicking in doors and accusing people of being vampires, especially the Founding Families."

"That's not my plan. We're going to kick in doors and burn down the ones who are vampires. No need to accuse. They give off a negative energy I can sense. Plus, if we catch them before sunset, it will be damn obvious what they are."

"Still. We can't barge into people's homes without a warrant."

I blinked at him. "What judge on this planet would issue a search warrant for vampires? And, the only thing a search warrant does is prevent evidence from being tossed out of court for an illegal search. None of what's about to happen in this town is going to end up in a courtroom. We're going to have piles of ash littered about that no one will be inclined to talk about."

Aaron chewed angrily at me. Yes, that's a thing. Chewing angrily at someone. A distorted noise came over the radio on his belt that sounded more like the sort of electronic nonsense ghost hunters captured and called EVPs than an actual person speaking. Then again, I'm throwing lightning bolts from my hands. I probably shouldn't dismiss the idea of ghosts as nonsense.

"Patty?" asked Aaron into the mic.

"Go ahead, Aaron."

"Did you hear any radio calls about forty minutes ago?"

"No. Sorry. It's a bit crazy here."

"Crazy how?" I asked.

"I thought some of the others were here, but I'm the only one in the building and we had a guy out front screaming about some kid breaking his car window with a rock. I had to deal with it myself. Radio was... unmanned for like fifteen minutes. I thought I kept an ear on it, but that guy was shouting right in my face like *I'm* the one who broke his damn window."

"There's no one else there?" asked Aaron.

"No. It's only me. Parker, Larson, and Ramirez didn't show up or call. Can't get them on the phone or radio. I'm pretty sure the others who should've been here today came in, but they've all vanished. Or maybe I only imagined seeing them."

Aaron stared at me with an expression like someone just stole his lunch. He clicked off his radio.

"My gut tells me that the vampires are changing tactics," I said, shoving the last of my burger in my mouth. "They're done pretending things in Shadow Pines are normal by mentally influencing the police, mayor, whoever else they had to. They're going to straight up take over. What happened to Justine probably happened to the rest of the deputies last night. Well, not so much being hung in a cage at the quarry—I mean... attacked. If they're lucky, they're dead."

"Dead is lucky?" Aaron tilted his head. "What's unlucky?"

"Becoming vampires themselves."

Chapter Six
Sense

Deputy Aaron Wilson appeared to find a second wind.

He shrugged off the exhaustion of being awake for a day and a half and rushed out to his patrol vehicle. Not wanting to leave him susceptible to vampiric attack, I raced after him. Crystal, presumably because she didn't want to leave *me* vulnerable, followed.

Maybe ten minutes away from my office, we screeched to a stop outside an apartment building. Aaron didn't say anything as he jumped out and ran for the entrance. Crystal and I followed. A nervous elevator ride later, we stepped out on the fifth floor. Upon noticing the door to apartment 5A ajar and broken, Aaron drew his Glock and crept closer.

He eased the door open and swept the room. "Aww, son of a…"

I stepped inside, catching a whiff of death. Yeah, they'd been here all right. The apartment looked like a WWE pay-per-view event had been filmed there. One floor lamp behind the couch lay on the floor, the glass shroud at the top smashed. Aaron hurried around to the front of the couch, shaking his head at the floor.

Speaking of death, a dead man sprawled on the rug in front of the television, his throat ripped open, killed pretty much the same way as Crystal's sister.

"Is that one of the deputies?" I whispered.

"Nah. But it's Ramirez's roommate, Jeff. Or was."

"That look like an animal attack to you?" I asked.

Aaron stared down, then shook his head. "Unless someone is teaching mountain lions how to pick locks now, then no."

"Do you see any blood?"

"Almost none. Wow. So, vampires are real, huh?"

For an answer, I clapped him on the shoulder and moved past the living room into the hallway. The smell of undead lingered in the back of the place, though it didn't stink strongly enough for me to worry about finding a vampire here right now. Of two bedrooms, one appeared undisturbed, the other had been tossed like a bar fight happened there. I'd only seen worse destruction at the Walmart in St. Collins a couple Black Fridays ago. No shell casings littered the rug, nor did I find any bullet holes. Guess Ramirez didn't sleep in arm's reach of a weapon or the attack had been too frenetic for him to get to it. Justine *was* a pretty light sleeper after all. I searched around several milk crate shelves, under the bed, under the pillow, on the desk… no sign of a gun. The vamps must've taken it when they took Ramirez.

Aaron appeared in the doorway, looked around, sighed. "Just checked the parking lot out back... Ramirez's car is still here."

"He's not in here, buddy. No blood or bullet holes. Seems like he put up somewhat of a fight, but they still got him."

"I can't…" Aaron's voice quivered as if he's about to cry. "None of this is making any sense. Paul Ramirez? The hell did he do to deserve this?" He let out a long sigh, eyes closed. "This has to be a crazy gang or some psycho targeting police."

I walked over and put a hand on his shoulder. "The first time someone tried to tell me vampires existed, I thought they were crazy. It took me seeing one for myself before I believed."

"This is bullshit!" roared Aaron, before punching a hole in the wall. "The sons of bitches who did this are freakin' dead."

Considering the guy shook with rage, I decided *not* to point out that his statement had been technically correct. "Okay. Run the IDs on the guys from the quarry. I guarantee you'll find normal citizens with no connections to each other or to any gang."

"That doesn't make any fucking sense." He paced a small circle, grabbed two fistfuls of hair.

I raised a light breeze circling the room, enough to make the curtains flutter and knock a few papers around. "Does this make sense?"

"I dunno, man. I dunno." Aaron wiped plaster dust off his knuckles. "No damn idea what the hell to do anymore."

Crystal walked up behind him. "Hey?"

He twisted to look at her. The instant they made eye contact, he stopped crying and calmed down. "Whoa."

"It's overwhelming, I know," she said soothingly. "But it's only overwhelming be-cause you're so used to being in a world where nothing like this is supposed to exist." She patted his cheek. "Max is trying to make Shadow Pines into the type of place where people can once again pretend this stuff isn't real. But he's going to need us to help him. Can you deal with the weird stuff for a little while longer? In a couple of days, you can pretend none of it really happened."

Aaron rubbed his forehead. "Yeah. Sorry about that. I'm so damn tired my brain's not working right. I've never gotten that emotional before."

"These are your friends. People you work with." I stopped the breeze. "It's totally understandable to have a moment like that."

"Why would they take Ramirez? Not to lure you into a trap." Aaron scowled at the wall.

"Doubtful. They are either giving him a mental command implant or want to turn him into a vampire."

Aaron shook with anger. "So he's dead?"

"If they intended to kill him, we would've found a body here."

"I meant dead like a vampire."

"Depends on if he's killed anyone," I said. "I have no damn idea how long it takes someone to get back up after they've been turned, but if we can destroy the one who made him into a vampire before he kills anyone, we can cure him."

Aaron stopped pacing, whirling to face me. "Are you just making this shit up as we go?"

"No. I've seen at least four proto-vampires who recovered after I destroyed their makers. You remember those three college kids found at the Shadow Pines Manor?"

"Yeah."

"Them. And one young woman just a day ago." I started for the door. "One thing that is not helping is standing around here and doing nothing."

"We gotta check on the others, Max."

"Okay, fine. But let's do it fast. Daylight is fading."

Chapter Seven
Needless

Aaron drove us to the residence of the next nearest missing deputy.

Don Larson had a house in a residential neighborhood known as Mill Heights southeast of the town center. Considerably older than the development with the morbid names, this area had a reputation as being 'the bad part of town.' For Shadow Pines, that meant sometimes the people who lived there let their lawn go a whole week overdue for a mowing. Sometimes, the weeds would pull knives on passing squirrels. Real serious stuff.

Deputy Larson's house looked like an old couple lived there. Powder blue, little flowerboxes on the front windows, tiny white fence around flowerbeds in front of the house. Oh, and gnomes. Ceramic ones, not actual gnomes. Good grief, I hoped those things weren't real.

Anyway, the driveway contained a late-Nineties Ford Explorer, black, plus a little white Toyota Celica. We didn't see any damage on the house's front door, so Aaron headed around to the backyard. Sadly, the back door had been ripped completely off. We went inside, conducted a quick search of the downstairs—which appeared normal except for the missing door—then went upstairs. Aaron took the lead, me behind him, Crystal last.

"Ugh," whispered Crystal at the top of the stairs. "There's a body."

I glanced back at her with a questioning eyebrow lift. She tapped her nose.

Aaron stopped in the doorway of the master bedroom, bowed his head, and muttered a few f-bombs in a row. "Why the hell did they do this?"

Jaw clenched, I edged up behind him.

A woman around forty lay dead upon the bed, so pale she had clearly been drained. Lifeless green eyes stared vacantly at the ceiling. A few drops of blood marked her nightgown. I couldn't say with any certainty if Deputy Don had been in the bed next to her. As with

Ramirez' place, the room showed no signs of gunfire, and no weapons lay out in sight. The back office closet had a gun safe big enough for rifles, but it hadn't been opened.

"Not much of a struggle happened here." I fussed at the bedding where Don would've been. "Doesn't really look like he was even here."

"Larson works the late shift. He wouldn't have gotten home until about five in the morning." Aaron broke down in tears again. "And he walks in to find his wife dead. Why would they kill Val?"

"They're vampires. That's the reason."

"It doesn't make any sense. If Don found his wife dead, he'd have the state police all over this place looking for the killer. Or at least, he'd have been screaming on the radio about it. Why go silent? What if he snapped and did this?"

I pointed at Val's ripped-open throat. "Unless he's already a vampire, I sincerely doubt he'd have chewed her throat wide open. Plus, there'd be a massive amount of blood soaked into the mattress."

"If the vampires intend to turn the police into their enforcers, they'd want to destroy any mortal attachments they'd have… like wives." Crystal sighed apologetically at Val.

Aaron grabbed his mic but didn't hit the talk

button. "So why would he disappear in silence like that? Think he might've seen Val dead and run off somewhere to end it?"

I shrugged. "Maybe if there was a place of special significance to him. More likely, if he wanted to be with her in the next world, he'd probably have laid down next to her and shot himself in the head."

"Yeah. True." Aaron exhaled and squeezed the mic. "Patty, it's Wilson. You still there?"

"Where else would I be?" replied the dispatcher.

"Just checked on Ramirez and Larson's home addresses. Found a homicide victim at both locations. I'm sorry to say, Val's dead."

"Oh, no…" Patty gasped.

"Look, I need to go check on Parker. If we still have a coroner, can you please send them here, and to Ramirez' apartment. Someone killed Paul's roommate. We got a psycho out there who declared war on us, Pat. I gotta find them."

"Copy, that."

Aaron looked at me in a way that said he expected to find the same thing at the next deputy's place. He approached the bed and rested his hand atop the corpse's. "We're gonna get the bastards, Val. I promise you."

Chapter Eight
Farmers

Deputy Chuck Parker lived in the truly crappy part of Shadow Pines, a little residential area about a quarter mile north of downtown.

It had nothing on the bad part of Ironside, but it *was* possible to get mugged here after dark. His house, a tiny one-bedroom thing not much bigger than a double-wide trailer, occupied a property stranded in limbo between a brown, dead lawn and dirt lot.

A small, round barbecue grill stood near the front porch, itself a tiny block of concrete with three steps and a bunch of cracks. This place must not have a back door since the front one appeared broken in.

Again, Aaron led the way inside. The living room took up the entire width of the place, a hallway leading back past a micro kitchen to a bedroom. Unless the closet-sized bathroom in the corner of the bedroom counted as separate, the house consisted of only three rooms. The kitchen had less space than my bathroom, so I doubted it counted as a real room, making this a two-room house. Really though, how much space did a single guy need?

Luckily, we didn't find anyone dead here.

Aaron stepped into the back to search the bedroom while I tried not to touch anything in the kitchen. I'd seen some filthy places in my life doing PI work, but I don't think Parker changed his trash bag in four years. Stacks of old ravioli cans stood on the counter nearly as tall as the ceiling. Judging by the mound of plates and crap in the sink, he never washed a single dish... ever. When he ran out, he started eating food straight from the cans—as evidenced by numerous cans with forks or spoons encrusted to them.

"Nothing here," said Aaron on the way out of the bedroom. "Parker's a bit of a slob. Can't tell if a fight happened in there or not."

"A bit?" I gestured at the countertop.

Aaron sighed and headed for the front door. We exited the house in single file. Crystal spun to the left a second before a man with dark brown hair and a sheriff's department uniform walked around the corner of the house. He regarded Aaron for only a second before looking at me.

"Chuck!" said Aaron. "Holy shit. Are you okay?"

"Fine. Why wouldn't I be?" Deputy Parker stared at me with this creepy out-to-lunch gaze.

"Because we're under attack. Someone's picking us off one by one—"

"Max! Look out!" yelled Crystal.

Chuck went for his sidearm, and so did Aaron. I briefly—and by that I mean for about $1/100^{th}$ of a second—considered knocking him over with a windblast, but didn't trust my ability to generate a strong enough gust in time. So, I dove for the doorway.

A rapid series of gunshots went off in the time between me jumping and landing flat on my chest in the living room. One car alarm wailed in the distance and several dogs erupted in a fit of barking.

"Fuck!" roared Aaron.

"Goddess," muttered Crystal.

I scrambled upright and peered outside.

Chuck lay dead on the ground, a dark bloodstain at the center of his shirt.

Most of the color had drained out of Aaron's

face. He still had his sidearm raised, arm slightly shaking. "I just killed Parker. God dammit."

Crystal stared at the body, blood spreading over the sidewalk. "He didn't give you any choice. He would have killed Max, then probably you as well. If he hadn't been going for Max first…"

"And I appreciate you having a hell of a fast draw," I said. And since Aaron appeared paralyzed, I went over to Chuck and nudged the Sig away from his hand with my foot.

"Soon as you said 'look out,' I noticed the emptiness in his eyes." Aaron holstered his sidearm. "That wasn't Chuck. In fact, it's the first time I didn't see him smiling. He might've been a hell of a slob, but he was always in a good mood. This here… it's like someone goddamned else had stolen his skin."

"They took Justine as bait and compelled this man to be an assassin. As soon as he saw Max, the mind control took over." Crystal massaged Aaron's shoulder. "I'm sorry you had to fire on a deputy, but you did the right thing. You didn't kill Parker. The vampires did."

Aaron pivoted to face me. "There has to be a better way to deal with this than killing them." He grabbed two fistfuls of my shirt and pulled me up on my toes. "Tell me we're not going to have to kill the rest of my friends."

Crystal's eyes flared open wider. His anger lessened in an instant and he let go of me.

"Yeah. There is a better way. Destroy the vampire or vampires responsible for the control and the control stops. We had less than a second here. You saved my ass. Don't blame Chuck for this, blame the fiends."

"I still…" He ran a hand up over his hair.

"Can't quite believe it's real? Yeah, I get it. Max Long of a few weeks ago would've been right there with you in Skeptic City."

"Crap." Aaron peeled his gaze up from the ground and made eye contact. "If they possessed Chuck, did they do the same to Sheriff Waters?"

"Yes, but they did that over a year ago. And they hadn't programmed her into an assassin, just a tool to help them hide their feeding or whatever else they wanted to get away with. The other day, I'm pretty sure she managed to break out." I shifted my jaw side to side while thinking. "It's possible they did it again. She sounded pretty angry with me, but her personality didn't go flat as soon as she saw me the way Chuck's had."

"Who are you that they're sending assassins after you?"

"Just an agent of Nature."

"Say again?"

"It's a long story... but I was chosen by Mother Nature herself to take care of the vampire problem. I am the yin to their yang, so to speak."

Aaron snapped his fingers. "The weird fire and wind."

"I have the elements at my disposal."

"The natural versus the supernatural."

I nodded, impressed. "Yes, sort of. Anyway, we need to consider that Justine might once again be under their influence."

"She won't be doing much for a week or two." Crystal shook her head. "She's going to spend the rest of today unconscious from surgery, then be too weak to get out of bed for a while. Even if she is a victim of mind control again, she won't be able to act on it before we take out the source. Even less chance of her doing anything if you stay out of her sight. If they're using trigger commands, as long as she doesn't see you, she'll remain herself."

"Who's doing this bullshit?" said Aaron, his voice veritably shaking. He'd taken to pacing again.

A few neighbors emerged from their houses to spectate.

"Vampires," I muttered.

Aaron nearly threw his gun into the sky, but

holstered it. "For what? What do they want?"

"Me dead. They know I'm dangerous to them."

Aaron gestured at Chuck. "But why are they attacking us? The police?"

"Probably due to what I said before. They're done pretending. They're going to take over the whole town and turn it into a feeding farm. Influencing Justine didn't help them enough, so maybe they're going to dominate *all* the deputies and use you as handlers to keep the human livestock in line. The situation in Shadow Pines has been steadily growing worse over the past year. Maybe this isn't a response to what we did at Wakefield Manor. They could have finally reached a point of power or number where they simply decided they no longer needed to pretend they didn't exist. Our town is isolated enough from the outside world for them to pull that off if they controlled information."

"I really hope not." Crystal folded her arms. "But does it matter why it's hit the fan? We've got two choices, boys: either we stamp them out or we let them take over."

"Screw that," said Aaron. "If those things *are* real, I say we blow the piss out of them."

"Agreed." I frowned at Chuck. "I feel like a dick for saying this, but we're wasting time checking on deputies. Three for three have been hit by vamps in the night. No reason to expect the rest haven't. We need to go after the fiends directly or more people are going to die like this."

"All right. Let me call this in and get the coroner out here, then we'll go wherever you think has the best chance of getting some god-damned revenge for Chuck." Aaron huffed, grabbed his mic, and took a few steps off to radio Patty.

I bowed my head.

"This isn't your fault either, Max." Crystal wrapped her arms around me.

"You know that part where the guy who's supposed to do the thing is having the 'why me' moment and doubting that he's the right man for the job? That's where I am right now."

"Maybe the answer is... just because."

I looked up at her. "Say again?"

"Why you? Because. You happened to be there. No reason beyond that."

"Could be." I chuckled. "Or maybe Mother Nature saw me for the international man of mystery I really am."

"Let's just stick with because."

I sighed. "So, you really think I didn't cause this? I mean Chuck's death, Val's death, the attacks on the deputies, the escalation of this war? Honestly? Or are you just saying that to make me feel better?"

"Ninety-ten. Something like this would have happened sooner or later, with or without you. Probably sooner."

"True." I rested my chin on her shoulder, drinking in her fragrance. "How much of Aaron's current calmness is coming from you?"

"Most of it. He's pretty angry and despondent right now. I'm encouraging him to stay level and not have a breakdown."

"Let him down easy later, okay?"

"Please." She playfully scoffed. "I know how to handle emotions."

Chapter Nine
Crime Scene

Aaron insisted on waiting for the coroner to show up.

I couldn't object to the delay despite my eagerness to make use of the remaining daylight so we could catch vampires sleeping. There's no such thing as *fair* in this war; after all, people didn't try to take up a fight with roaches on even terms. Besides, we couldn't just leave Chuck lying there to be gawked over by the growing number of curious locals attracted by the gunshots.

Meanwhile, Aaron drifted back and forth between seeming on the verge of a mental breakdown and holding it together. He rambled about how Sheriff Waters would've sent him back to the station, or even home, and had other deputies secure the shooting scene. Cops didn't run around like cowboys, shooting friends, then continuing on with their day hunting vampires.

But Shadow Pines had a crisis. With Justine in the hospital, that left Aaron Wilson as the town's *only* apparently functional law enforcement person. Even if he did call in the state police, they'd have to come in from St. Collins, a forty-five minute ride away. Besides, they'd only get in the way… and didn't deserve to be dragged into this vampire crap. Basically, we had no one else to come take over so he didn't have to stand there staring at a former friend he'd killed. Crystal continually reassured him that Chuck hadn't snapped or gone insane. Aaron had no reason not to remember his friend in anything but a positive way.

Hell of a thing for any man to deal with, much less on only a few hours' sleep.

A white van with 'medical examiner' on it arrived eighteen minutes after he called it in. Like I said, Shadow Pines had an unusual amount of money for a small town. Few cities this size had their own medical examiner's office. Then again, our coroner also served Ironside. Aaron rather skillfully explained that the deputies ended up severely short-staffed and he needed to chase down a lead regarding the murder of Valerie Larson. The skinny blond guy who drove the coroner's van appeared stunned when told most of the sheriff's department had gone missing.

While the man photographed the body, Aaron walked back over to Crystal and me.

"Ready?" I asked.

"Almost. Once Ned has Chuck in the van, we can go."

"All right. You okay?"

Aaron gave a mirthless laugh. "No. But I'm functioning. It's messed up, but if those vampires turn out to be real, I think it will make me feel a lot better. Right now, I still don't know what the hell to believe."

"Won't be long now until you see one. Your gun isn't going to do much good. Might want to find a sword."

He blinked at me. "I have no idea how the hell to fight with a sword."

"Easy." Crystal smiled. "You stick the sharp end into them until they stop moving. Sword play only requires skill and training if you're going up against someone else with a sword. Otherwise, it's more like carving a turkey... well, a turkey that's running around in circles and can kill you."

"Great. Sounds like fun." Aaron gazed off at

the sky. "We got a couple hours of daylight left. Assuming vampires exist, what's our next move?"

"Try to catch as many asleep as we can. Probably at Farrington Manor or the Blackwood Estate. Both of those families have significant connections to the undead." I spat to the side.

"I dunno." Aaron fidgeted. "Connections or not, those two families have a lot of clout. It's nearly impossible for us to even give them a parking ticket without causing a political incident."

"Lucky for me, I don't care about politics." I wagged my eyebrows.

Crystal put a hand on my arm. "Let's go back to the Wakefield mansion and look around."

"What for? The place is empty."

"Exactly. The whole family except for Blair was undead. There might be information there about other vampires. Remington was mentally stuck in the 1800s, remember? He's probably kept a journal by hand, not in a computer."

I hopped in the back again, letting Crystal have the passenger seat. On the way to the manor, we got into a discussion about the effectiveness of bullets on vampires. So far, I had little faith that shooting a fiend would do a damn thing, but Crystal thought putting a bullet in their heads would roughly equate to a knockout punch. It wouldn't destroy them, but might keep them out of commission for a while.

"So cutting their head off with a sword destroys them, but shooting them in the brain doesn't?" asked Aaron.

"If you want to split hairs, simply cutting their heads off doesn't kill them either," said Crystal. "It makes them inert for a really long time. Eventually, they'd recover. Faster if another vampire puts their head back on for them. To truly kill them, they have to be burned —or exposed to sunlight... unless you've got a silver sword. Pretty sure that would kill them right away, but I don't think anyone has ever made a sword out of pure silver. The metal is too soft." She gestured at me. "But we don't have to worry about that since we've got a ready source of fire."

"What about a shotgun? If their entire brain is on the wall, will that do the trick?" asked Aaron.

She winced.

"It'll put them to sleep long enough for me to get around to lighting them on fire." I smiled. "So, effective."

"Good enough," said Aaron.

Chapter Ten
A Bunch of Hooey

Even in the daylight, Wakefield Manor had an imposing presence that made me feel like we'd driven straight into a horror movie. The sort of film where a dozen people went into a house and only one bloody young woman crawled out at the end... and maybe still died when the one conveniently surviving monster shows up. Pretty sure this place had a pool somewhere, and I wouldn't be going anywhere near it. If blood started seeping from the walls, I'd just as soon burn the entire house down.

When we'd left the other day, the courtyard contained about a dozen expensive cars, Mercedes, BMWs, Maseratis, and so on. They remained, but three much less impressive cars had joined them. Either some curious locals had come to explore the place or word had already spread among the undead about what happened here.

"Who do you think belongs to those cars?" I asked.

"The normal-looking ones?"

"Yeah."

Aaron squinted at them. "All out of town plates." He ran them on the laptop next to him. "Nothing in the system on them about being stolen."

"Out of town? Probably vamps. Killed some tourists and took their cars." I opened the door, stepped out, and stared up at the house.

"They don't usually kill outsiders." Crystal gave me a worried stare. "That could mean they're getting more aggressive."

"Or are less concerned with consequences." I shoved the Tahoe's door shut and faced the mansion like a gunslinger about to have a showdown.

The house seemed to be glaring back at me as if to say 'bring it.' Maybe Crystal had been on to something with her suggestion we come back here. The idea of a primary 'source' being responsible for the situation in Shadow Pines took root in my brain ever since we snuck onto the grounds the other night. This place gave off energy like nowhere else around here. Dark, twisty energy that did unkind things to my psyche… like making me feel seven years old again and wanting to call out for my father to check under the bed for monsters. On second thought, no. This energy was a *lot* darker.

Aaron didn't seem to notice it at all, but he neither possessed elemental magic, werewolf blood, or fey heritage. I hoped the place had a much less pronounced effect on normal people, since that meant it would've been easier on Blair. If that kid had even a quarter of the reaction I did to this place, being locked in a room and unable to get away from that darkness should have driven her out of her mind. Crystal said she felt fear on the girl even if she didn't show any, but that didn't necessarily prove what appeared to be a child was, in fact, a child.

Yeah, I'm questioning everything… even the part about her being a kid. Must be this damn mansion… already playing havoc with my head.

That said, nothing about Blair—other than her being trapped here—had bothered me. Granted, eerie calm did bug me, but shock could do odd things. Some people didn't react to horrific events until hours or even days later. If Crystal hadn't vouched for the girl's emotions being genuine, I'd already be racing back to the Bradbury estate to… I dunno… fling holy water on Blair or something.

We made our way inside, Aaron having armed himself with his shotgun. Not wanting to be ambushed from behind, I went straight to the kitchen and the stairs down to the basement. If, indeed, stray vampires came here sensing a nice new lair, they'd be as far from the sunlight as possible. Better we destroy them before they woke up.

Of course, we hadn't seen anything down in the part of the basement we'd been in even close to resembling beds or coffins, though vampires didn't really do that. Sleeping in coffins came entirely from Hollywood. If any vampires actually did that, it would purely be for melodrama. However, we hadn't explored the entire basement, only the most direct route to the stairs up. That basically left roughly half of it unexplored. Aaron and Crystal followed me down the stairs without a word. Predictably, the light switch didn't do anything.

I created a ball of fire in my hand to see, careful to keep it away from the dusty sheet-covered furniture down here. One cobweb in the wrong place could spell disaster. Humanity had evolved away from carrying torches for a good reason. Then again, as easily as I could create fire, I could also put it out. So… no real need for concern.

Within a moment of stepping off the bottom stair, the unmistakable stench of rot slapped me in the face. I paused and put a hand on Aaron's arm before making a 'shh' gesture. He appeared confused, so I tapped my nose, then made a 'fang' gesture with my fingers. The face he made at that could've been suspicion as easily as nervousness. Either way, I'm sure I looked ridiculous.

The stink led me to the right, in the opposite direction from the Alcatraz-style jail cells where we'd found Jackson. After navigating enough old furniture to outfit a new hotel, we found a thick door reinforced with metal bands. It seriously looked like something out of a medieval castle, made of four-by-fours riveted together. A pissed-off werewolf probably wouldn't have been able to break it down.

Crystal gingerly tried the knob, smiled in a 'yeah, thought so' sort of way, then flicked the lock plate near the keyhole. A faint *click* came from inside. Aaron gawked at her as she turned the knob and struggled to pull the massive thing open. I grabbed the edge of the four-inch-thick door and helped.

Beyond lay a chamber divided into separate 'rooms' by old-timey folding privacy barriers, mostly gold and red velvet, some black, some purple… the sort of things movies always put in Wild West brothels. Crystal opened her purse and pulled her sword out. Aaron stared at the medieval longsword emerging from a bag that in no way should have been able to hold it. Crystal's purse was on the large side, more a satchel really, but certainly not four feet deep. Maybe I should've warned him she carried a reality-defying purse.

I peered around barriers one after the next at empty beds. The 'rooms' had varying degrees of personalization. Some appeared as sparse as a prison cell while others resembled the way bedrooms might've looked 150 years ago. The fifth one I checked appeared to have belonged to a woman based on the décor. A small night-stand beside the bed had a framed picture of Blair from roughly two years ago. The photo would have been adorable if eight-year-old Blair didn't have an expression that suggested she'd been terrified to turn her back on her own mother.

Aww, dammit. I didn't need to see something that humanized vampires. Maybe her mother *had* retained some trace of parental love, but I couldn't accept that. The woman allowed her daughter to be treated like a prisoner. And sure, kids could be rebellious, but when a child younger than ten ties a rope of bed sheets to her barred third-story window and climbs out to escape *multiple times*, that's a bit more of a red flag than cutting school.

Two 'rooms' later, we found the pallid corpse of a late-twenties guy reclining on a bed. His clothing, a normal T-shirt and jeans, didn't say much about his potential age as a vampire, but it didn't matter.

I gave Aaron a 'here we go' look, then raised both hands.

The fiend's eyes snapped open an instant before the fist-sized fireball I'd made for light stretched forward into a flamethrower stream. He went up like a pile of dry matchsticks, managing to fling his burning self upright. Fangs bared, he let off a hiss, then a growl too deep to have come from any human throat. He tried to lunge at me, but collapsed to the floor three steps from the bed, his body falling apart and disintegrating to ashes in mere seconds.

Answering hisses came from elsewhere in the basement.

Aaron gawked.

"Believe me now?" I asked, stepping back into the 'corridor' between barriers.

Much to my surprise, Aaron smiled. It seemed that seeing clear proof his friend Chuck hadn't really turned into a murderer helped him convert guilt into anger at the vampires.

A woman in a halter top and short skirt came flying out of the darkness toward us. I'd have called her pretty, but fangs and glowing red eyes didn't do it for me. I started to gather fire, but an unexpected blast from Aaron's shotgun caught me off guard, breaking my focus. The magic in my hand fizzled out in a puff of smoke.

She went from running to sliding in an instant, her face a mangled ruin.

Crystal let out a scream, more of a war cry. I spun to my right as she hacked her sword into the head of a vampire who'd come up behind her. She'd tried to decapitate him but missed, instead burying the edge into his cheek and slicing three-quarters of the way through his skull. Another vampire raced at us from the left. The manic fury in his eyes was a far more immediate concern than gawking at the one Crystal mangled.

I bathed him in a stream of fire at the same time Aaron shot him in the face. The vampire melted into a cloud of ashes before his body hit to the floor. Crystal leaned back and stomp-kicked her vampire in the chest, flinging him off her blade. He grabbed the upper part of his head, trying to prevent it from breaking off—at least until she swung for his throat. The fiend hurled himself out of the way, avoiding her attack, but the abrupt motion snapped the little bit of bone holding the top half of his head in place. It fell off, wobbling like a dropped bowl while the rest of him went into a convulsing fit.

"Eww." Crystal cringed away.

Fire put him out of our misery.

"Damn. These things *are* real," whispered Aaron, staring at the late-twenties woman he'd shot. "Aww, fuck me."

"I don't think she's interested," muttered Crystal.

"No…" He crouched over her corpse and held her limp arm up to show off a bracelet made of four parallel rows of gold chain and jade beads. "This belonged to Val."

The woman lurched upward, biting him on the shin with what remained of her jaw. He screamed more out of surprise than pain, hopping backward while trying to kick her off his leg. Crystal sliced the fiend's head off, and I lit the remains on fire as soon as Aaron distanced himself.

"That woman had a hole through her face as big as a drainpipe… and was still alive." Aaron shifted his wild-eyed gaze to me.

"You hurt?" I pointed at the blood smear on his leg. "And if you want to be technical, she wasn't alive. Vampires are undead."

He glanced down at himself. "No… didn't

break skin. I think the shotgun blast broke her fangs."

"Didn't have much of a jaw left either." I shuddered, then sighed. "So much for easy pickings."

"How's that?" He pumped the shotgun, ejecting a still-smoking empty shell.

"It's still daylight out, but they woke up to come after us. I had hoped they'd lay there like logs and let me ignite them one by one."

"A little more sporting this way," said Aaron.

I might have rolled my eyes. Crystal poked another barrier aside with her sword and peered past it. "They have a kind of survival instinct. We just witnessed them at their most feral."

"Is that good or bad?" asked Aaron.

"Both." She lowered her sword arm and faced him. "Bad because they're stronger, faster, and entirely devoid of fear. Good because they lack any ability to think when they're forced awake before sunset. Little more than wild dogs."

I nodded, fully agreeing with that assessment.

"Squatters," said Crystal. "These weren't Wakefields."

"That one"—Aaron pointed at the ash pile around the bracelet—"either killed Val or was there."

"Good chance of that, yeah. Or maybe one of them gave it to her." I kept going down the 'hall' between rooms, looking around. Curiously, the dark energy pervading this entire estate grew stronger the deeper I went. The vamps probably wouldn't have kept a mortal captive in their inner sanctum, but I had to at least check. "Whether she did or didn't kill Val, one of this group did and they're all gone now."

Aaron kicked at the ashes. "Rest in peace, Valerie."

Eventually, I reached an actual wall—as opposed to a collapsible barrier—as wide as the entire basement. A single door at the middle led into a massive room decorated with ancient furniture. If not for the absence of windows, it might've been an ordinary room above ground. The décor made me feel as if I'd gone back in time to the 1830s, except for a complete lack of lamps. Not even an oil-burning lantern or candles. That came as no surprise. Vampires could see in total darkness, and they certainly wouldn't want fire anywhere near them.

A few minutes into searching the place, I knew two things. One: Remington Wakefield enjoyed reading, as evidenced by the entire innermost wall covered in tall bookshelves. Two: they hadn't kept any human prisoners in here. I sifted among the papers on the desk while Crystal checked out the bookshelves. Aaron shined a flashlight around, whistling to himself. My hopes of finding a ledger or Rolodex of vampires died. If any such records existed, Remington hadn't left them out in the open. In most movies and stories, rooms like this always had secret passages. Maybe he had a wall safe hidden behind a painting or bookshelf. Only an idiot would leave documentation about vampires out in the open after all.

Thinking back to the way I'd sensed the mass grave of seniors in the forest off Minepath Road, I opened myself to the presence of the earth. The instant my senses perceived the room around me as a void surrounded by dirt and stones, another void extended forward behind the bookshelves, connected by a short, square corridor. I approached the bookshelf by the tunnel, looking over various titles that appeared to be fiction novels. Most of these books appeared quite old, likely from the era of physical print presses. As in Gutenberg-style print presses.

"Crystal?"

"Hmm?" She walked over.

"I'm sensing a passage here. Do you have any skills at finding secret, ah, mechanisms?"

"I'm not a thief, but I do have sharp eyes.

The cliché thing would be a fake book that acts as a switch."

"What would the non-cliché thing be?" I asked.

She laughed. "We're already looking for a secret passageway, so we're past the point of not being in a cliché. But I suppose the sneakier way to conceal the mechanism would be somewhere in the decorative carvings on the shelves. Perhaps one of the berries or leaves is a button."

The three of us spent a few minutes searching that bookshelf before Crystal discovered the way in. A carved cherub with a head the size of a plum had a trick wing. Pulling its right wing forward acted like a handle and allowed the bookshelf to swing out from the wall.

A wave of what I could only describe as tangible evil washed over me as the shelf passed by. If I had been alone, no doubt existed in my mind that I'd have screamed and run like a little boy. The notion that the fear came from my brain possessing no good way to translate the interaction of positive and negative energy— plus having Crystal and Aaron there—let me hold my ground.

The world consisted of both positive and negative forces. Far fewer monsters existed than people, so each of them had a greater portion of negative energy than humans had positive energy. This resulted in vampires having super-natural powers people didn't. Mom Nature had seen fit to 'supercharge' me, which likely made me more susceptible to noticing the presence of my opposite force.

"I think we found it…" I whispered.

"Found what?" asked Aaron.

"The source."

Crystal took my arm. She, too trembled. We exchanged a glance. Upon realizing we both shook like frightened children, we managed to calm down.

"The source?" Aaron raised an eyebrow.

"Yes," I said. "The reason there are so many vampires gathered in Shadow Pines."

Oh, hell. I'd been chosen to deal with this problem. Time to trust in my abilities. Rather, time to trust in Mother Nature. I clenched my jaw and walked in.

The short stone corridor led to another chamber only a little smaller than Remington's bedroom. Dark grey walls of plain stone surrounded a mostly empty space with no furnishings other than an altar of sorts in the middle of a ritual circle painted on the floor. I couldn't even begin to guess at the meanings of the various squiggles and symbols, but it wasn't a pentagram at least. Nowhere—not in movies, books, or reality—had I ever seen this kind of thing before.

We approached the altar at the same time, pausing a step away.

A large bowl contained a quantity of what appeared to be blood with a human eyeball, one finger, and a rat's head floating in it. Next to it lay an ornate dagger, its gold handle carved in the shape of a coiled dragon. Several candles, a human skull, multiple papers, and three dingy cloth bundles of unknown contents also sat upon the altar.

"You've gotta be freakin' kidding me," said Aaron. "Satanists?"

"No, this isn't Satanism." Crystal walked around the altar, examining the stuff. "It's not witchcraft either. I can't even begin to guess what happened here, but the energy in this room is overwhelmingly bad."

"That's usually how I feel when Sheriff Waters screams at me to go to her office." Aaron gave a weak laugh. "So this crap is the real deal? Are you going to tell me horoscopes are legit?"

"I wouldn't quite go that far."

Crystal rolled her eyes. "Please. I don't know how anyone can believe planets affect our destiny. Such nonsense. If people really wanted to know what the future held for them, they'd use crystals, like a proper fey."

Aaron and I exchanged a glance.

"This is... terrifying." Aaron shook his head... and kept on shaking it.

I reached for the bowl, but jammed my fingers into an invisible barrier. "Ow, crap!"

"What?" asked Aaron.

"There's some kind of... shield here." I tried again, more slowly, and patted an invisible bubble around the altar. Neither cold nor warm, it had the smoothness of glass, a seamless sphere around the entire altar all the way down to the floor. Touching it prickled at my skin, painfully enough that I flinched back, wincing.

Crystal patted it, feeling its shape out. "Oh, wow. I've never seen—or felt—anything like this before."

"Says the girl who can teleport." I chuckled.

"You guys are messing with me. There's nothing there."

I glanced at Aaron. "Try to pick up that bowl."

"That's disgusting."

"Okay, try to pick up the knife."

Smirking, he reached for the altar—and banged his hand on the barrier. "Aw, shit."

"See?" I asked.

Aaron made a face like someone had poured lukewarm oatmeal down the back of his pants as he prodded the invisible bubble. "Okay, where's the camera?"

"What camera?" asked Crystal.

"This is some kind of elaborate 'welcome back from vacation' prank." Aaron folded his arms. The look in his eye suggested the man might be close to losing it. "Val's not dead. Chuck's not dead. None of this crap is real. You're some kind of expensive prank company, right? All this vampire and magic stuff is a giant pile of hooey."

Except the man had killed his fellow deputy and friend not more than an hour ago. He was losing it, that much was obvious. I placed a gentle hand on his shoulder. "Sorry, Aaron. This is as real as it gets. Might be unbelievable, but it's the truth."

"A frickin' force field?" He pounded the butt of the shotgun at the bubble. Oddly, it didn't make any noise, merely stopped short in midair. "Oh, this is so weird. And no... I get it. Just hoping maybe saying it's all BS out loud might make it true that none of it's real."

Crystal pulled her phone out and snapped several pictures of the altar. "Mother doesn't deal with this kind of mysticism, but she might at least be able to identify what school it came from and what its purpose is."

"Wasn't Nigel Farrington an arcanist?" I

asked, eyebrows furrowed.

"Yes, but we're under the *Wakefield* Manor." Crystal glanced at me, then took another picture. "I'm not sure they'd have let him in here. Remington became a vampire before Nigel was born. But, I suppose, it's possible. Sometimes the Founding Families do work together when it means a great deal of power or money for both sides that they can't get alone."

"I am completely clueless when it comes to 'magic,'" I said, "But, if I had to guess, I'd say that whatever this is, it's either attracting vampires to the area or making them stronger. This altar thing has to be important. The Wakefields were the only family to entirely give themselves to vampirism and this is in their basement. It has to be connected."

"Agreed," said Crystal. "But Nigel died to an 'animal attack' not long ago."

Aaron scoffed, seemingly back to his normal, cynical self. "Animals... wow. All this time that's been vampires?"

"Fair bet, yeah." I poked at the force bubble, still mystified that such a thing could exist. "Nigel's unfortunate encounter with a mountain lion... was that your grandmother's doing?" I glanced at Crystal.

"Likely called in a favor, yes." She put her

phone back in her bag. "I think the old one was actually somewhat upset they wanted to abduct and kill me." She was, of course, referring to the man who'd arranged Dana's murder as a way to lure Crystal back to Shadow Pines. He'd wanted to kill her and use her fey soul to power some kind of magical ring or some such thing. Honestly, I hadn't believed it fully back then. But, seeing a force field...

"Surprising that she'd care," I said. "You're no blood relation of Darth Grandmother." The old one was Sterling Bradbury's mother. Crystal's actual father came from another dimension.

She shrugged. "True. But Anna Bradbury hated me because she thought I'd seduced her son, who everyone thought was my father. No sense keeping that cat in a bag now. Once she learned it had been Brittany Anworth he'd cheated on Mother with, I think she respected me for protecting his reputation. Perhaps even endeared me to her... a little."

I rubbed my forehead. In what world did allowing family members to think a father took his daughter to bed end up being *better* for his reputation than sleeping with someone from the 'wrong family.' I will never understand high society.

"I think I'd have more trouble believing Darth Grandmother smiled than vampires existed." I winked at her.

Crystal snickered. "She's not as dour as she looks. There's nothing more we can do here right now. Let's show these pictures to Mother and maybe she can give us something that can penetrate this bubble."

"Why do we want to penetrate the bubble?" asked Aaron.

"While I don't understand this particular practice of spellcraft, ritual magic has certain laws that transcend discipline." Crystal gestured at the altar. "If anything is changed, even moving a candle a half inch, it could disrupt the effect of the magic, which is likely why there's an energy bubble protecting it. Sweeping everything off the altar entirely has a good chance of ending the spell."

"And that's a good thing?" asked Aaron.

"Yes." She blinked at me. "A spell made by vampires in the basement of a mansion full of them could only have a bad purpose."

"You sound nervous." I peered over the altar at her. "What else might happen?"

"Um…" She bit her lip. "If we do the wrong thing, whatever entity is at the other end of this spell could become angry. Or we could simply release the energy of the ritual into… an explosion."

"Entity?" asked Aaron. "Explosion?"

"The markings in the circle make me think that this ritual is acting like a bridge to another dimension. It is allowing energy from that dimension to cross into ours. Something that lives on the other side is either the anchor point over there or the patron, like begging power from a dark god."

Aaron edged away from the altar. "If you're about to tell me we're going to end up fighting Cthulhu or some shit like that, I'm going back to Florida."

"Oh, no. That's fictionalized," said Crystal, shaking her head. "At least, as far as I know, the things referred to as 'gods' are not quite as cataclysmically powerful as the term 'god' would suggest. They have their limits and it's not completely impossible for mere humans to beat one... just rather difficult. We should hurry. Daylight is fading. If there is any intelligence behind this, it's going to seek to protect itself. This room could be wall-to-wall vampires as soon as the sun's down. And if we want to wait for tomorrow morning, we're going to need to find a place we can defend from an army... because they're going to let us have it tonight."

"You make it sound so easy." I winked.

"It is easy. *If* we get lucky." She wagged her eyebrows. "Let's go."

Chapter Eleven
A Matter of Urgency

After a brief trip to verify no unlucky people had wound up trapped in the Wakefield's prison cells, we headed outside to Aaron's truck and drove to the Bradbury mansion.

It took us about sixteen minutes due to winding rural roads connecting both estates to downtown on opposite sides of the city, plus a traffic snarl. Upon our arrival at the mansion, Aaron parked close to the front steps, ignoring that it hadn't been designed as a place for people to put vehicles. We got out and hurried after Crystal, who seemed in an unusual hurry.

She shoved the front door open and called out for her mother on the way into the foyer.

"Sophia is not here, miss." Pierce emerged from a side hall and glided over to us.

"What? Why not?" Crystal spun to stare at him. "Where would she go?"

He nodded in greeting to me and Aaron, his expression worried-but-calm. "A pair of deputies arrived earlier, saying they needed to take young Blair for a mandatory interview with social services. Your mother is proceeding with a formal adoption, and the authorities insisted the girl be evaluated. They've been gone a few hours now."

"Shit," I whispered.

Crystal whipped her phone out and tried to call her mother. "Straight to voicemail."

"Shit," I repeated.

Aaron grabbed his shoulder mic. "Patty, it's Aaron, come back?"

"Go ahead, Aaron."

"You have anything in the log about our people going out to the Bradbury place to collect a minor for social services?"

"Nope. I already told you, no one's here. I thought I heard some of the guys earlier, but the station's a ghost town now."

"Dammit!" shouted Crystal, tears gathering in her eyes. She concentrated for a few seconds and appeared to gain a measure of calm. "Mother's okay."

"Where is she?" I grasped her arm.

"Not sure. I can tell she's alive, but not where she is." Crystal looked around for a few seconds before her expression lit up with an idea. "Wait here a minute."

Before I could say a word, she vanished out of her clothes, which settled to the floor where she'd been standing. As long as I live, that will never *not* unnerve me.

"Gah!" shouted Pierce.

"Guess he believes in teleporting now too." Aaron chuckled.

"Oh, no, young man." Pierce smiled at him. "We're quite aware of young Miss Bradbury's special talents. It merely shocked me that she's being… inappropriate. Was one thing as a small child when she had no control, but she knows better now. At least, I'd like to think so."

"Inappropriate?" I asked.

"Traipsing about the house undressed." Pierce fanned himself.

"My good man," I said, adopting a fake (and bad) British accent. "You do realize she's part succubus."

"Yes, yes. I am well aware. Such things are to be expected of her, but that doesn't mean they aren't impolite in proper society."

Yeah, but hiring vampire assassins and disowning children over fake scandals are perfectly 'polite.'

Aaron jumped back. "Where did she go?"

"Good question," I said.

A minute or so later, Crystal reappeared. Pierce gasped and averted his gaze. Aaron drank her in with his eyes. Sure, I felt a bit jealous, but I couldn't blame the guy for staring. This girl could practically make a dead man turn his head as she walked by.

"Got it! She's at the Sheriff's Department. Come on, we have to hurry!" Crystal picked up her clothes, shoes, and purse, then sprinted outside, carrying them.

"She's…" Aaron pointed at her streaking across the courtyard to the Tahoe.

"Yes, she is. Crystal's got an interesting, um, personality."

He blinked. "I could cite her for indecent exposure."

"Yeah, but you won't. Come on." I briefly glanced at the butler, said, "Thanks, Pierce," and dashed after her with Aaron following behind.

Outside, Crystal had already climbed into the back seat, slamming the door. Aaron and I ran over and got in, too. While he drove us out onto the long private road connecting the estate to the public street, she proceeded to get dressed.

"How do you know where your mother is?" I asked.

"Went upstairs to check her computer. She's got a program on it to track her cell phone. Mom's not great with technology. She loses her phone three times a week."

"You teleported upstairs?" I laughed. "What did you save about… twenty seconds?"

"It's a big house. More like two minutes, but my Mother is in danger. Two minutes could matter."

"Why not teleport to the Sheriff's Office?" asked Aaron.

"Just because everyone thinks I was a juvenile delinquent doesn't mean it's true. I've only been there once, as you well know, and contrary to what gossip would have you believe, not against my will. And I don't imagine the sheriff's department would appreciate me streaking around… at least not while I'm visible. Besides, if it hits the fan, I don't want to jump into the middle of a bad situation unarmed."

Yeah, she couldn't exactly say out loud that I'd asked her to go rifle through Justine's office while invisible in front of Aaron. Supernatural or not, it's still rather illegal. I twisted in my seat to smile at her, grinning at the way she fluffed her hair out the neck of her T-shirt while putting it on. "Since when does not being dressed bother you?"

"It doesn't. It bothers everyone else. Honestly, the clothes I couldn't care less about. I want my sword and knives. You're lucky, Max. You're never without your best weapon against them. Please"—she patted Aaron on the shoulder—"go faster."

He accelerated... and kept on accelerating.

Chapter Twelve
Missing Key

We arrived at the Sheriff's department six minutes later.

Aaron screeched the Tahoe to a stop in one of the official parking spaces. We scrambled out and ran to the station's front entrance. No desk sergeant greeted us. The whole building appeared empty. However, faint shouting and banging came from an inner hallway. Crystal took off like a bullet, running in that direction. Aaron and I tried our best to keep up with her, but the girl could *move*. Soon, the distant voice clarified to Sophia Bradbury shouting for someone to open the door.

I followed the commotion to a hallway

containing several secure interview rooms. Crystal, already at the last room on the left side, tapped the doorknob, magically unlocking it. As she yanked the door open, her mother spilled out of the room.

"What are you doing here?" Sophia stared at Crystal for a few seconds before grabbing her in a fierce hug. "Never mind! They took her!"

"The Sheriff's Department is compromised," I said, jogging up to them. "Aaron here is the only one we know for sure is free of vampire influence."

Crystal spun to glare at him. "Do we? Know that for sure I mean? He could've been affected before he went to Florida. The vamps have been here for years."

"Umm." Aaron's expression went blank. "I don't remember ever doing anything against my will or having any like blackouts or strange experiences."

Sophia, red eyed as though she'd been crying for a while, stared at him for a long moment. "He's fine, I don't sense any attachments. More importantly—they took Blair! The two deputies asked me to wait in here, but they locked the door and ran off with her. I've been banging on that door and screaming for hours."

"Why the heck would they want her?" I asked. "More bait?"

"Possibly, since the trap they tried to set with Justine didn't work. However, it could be related to what we found in the basement." Crystal took out her phone. "Mother, what do you make of this? It had some kind of 'shield' around it. We couldn't touch anything on the altar."

Sophia frowned, looked at the phone. "You found this in the basement?"

"Under the Wakefield house," said Crystal.

"Always figured the Founders were kinda eccentric," said Aaron, "but I never expected exactly how much."

Sophia nodded. "Yes, the strange energy I felt on her makes sense now. Blair, as a Wakefield, is probably tied to that ritual. Magic of that nature tends to follow family lines."

"She inherited it?" asked Crystal. "Does that mean she can control it? The magic, I mean."

"Not exactly." Sophia continued staring at the photographs.

I gestured at the phone. "Any chance that this might be what's responsible for summoning the darkness to Shadow Pines? The same way seeing vampires fills me with a need to destroy them, I want to smash that altar. That's gotta be Mom Nature telling me what to do."

"Yes." Sophia swiped to the next image. "I'm not familiar with this exact discipline, though it bears resemblance to a few strains of occultism that originated in Eastern Europe in the late 1700s. Some traditions are so dark that even the slightest bit of study tempts one to go deeper, and before you know it, your mind— and soul—are lost. I'll need more time to evaluate this and try to determine what the exact nature of the ritual is."

"But you have a general understanding for how a ritual like this works?" I asked.

Her smile came off as slightly patronizing. "Of course. And I will say this: Blair is probably the only person who that barrier will allow to pass."

Crystal's jaw dropped. "Are you telling us that Blair is seriously the only person who can stop this?"

"I can't say for sure about 'stopping this,' but she is quite likely the only one here at the moment who can disrupt the altar. I have no idea what will happen after she does that. The energy I sensed in her must be coming from this ritual. If there is anyone in Shadow Pines who can break that enchantment, it's her. But, you can't let anything happen to her."

"The vampires, or at least their thrall cops, have her." I let out a heavy sigh. "What happens if she, umm…"

"Dies?" asked Sophia, shaking her head.

"Terrible as that would be, the barrier would most likely become impenetrable unless another mass sacrifice is conducted. And that might not even work. Someone who is familiar enough with whatever magical tradition made this ritual in the first place would need to conduct a counter ritual. I'm taking an educated guess here based on the look of things, but between four to eight people were probably murdered during the initial spell. You'd need to kill at least four more to enact an unwinding spell powerful enough to break that ritual... *if* you can find a mystic with knowledge of the correct tradition."

"So what you're saying is..." I raised an eyebrow. "If anything happens to Blair, we're completely f—"

Crystal put a hand over my mouth. "You're talking to my mother."

I nodded. She lowered her arm.

"And to answer your question, Max," said Sophia. "Yes... we'd be completely effed if some-thing happened to her. And I'm not simply overstating that because I don't want her hurt."

"Well, there's no way I'm going to be able to murder innocent people, even to stop this mess," I said. "There has to be another way."

"Without her, there is—as far as I know—

only one way to destroy that altar." Sophia shivered with worry. "Our only other option would be constantly fighting new vampires that came here like bugs to a zapper."

Aaron laughed. "That might not be a bad idea. Leave the stupid thing there and kill them as they show up."

I faced him. "And what do we do if a hundred show up at once? It's too damn dangerous. We have to find that kid."

"Yes!" shouted Sophia. "Sorry, I've grown quite fond of her lately. Ritual or not, please don't let them hurt her. She's been through so damn much. She doesn't deserve this."

"Wait," said Crystal. "That doesn't make sense."

"What doesn't?" Sophia blinked.

"If killing her would make their spell indestructible, why haven't they already done it? The vampires—Wakefields—had her locked up for ten years." Crystal held her arms out to either side. "Why didn't they kill her already?"

"Perhaps because she was their family?" asked Sophia.

"They hadn't been her family for eight years. Merely creatures who looked like her family." I tapped my foot, frustrated at not having answers, but knowing Crystal was on to something here. "Could that ritual bind to vampires the way it's linked to her? Maybe she wouldn't have been so important while the remainder of the Wakefield family continued to exist as vampires?"

Crystal nodded. "But being the last of the Wakefields... makes her damn important now."

"Which is why the vampires are trying to protect her," added Aaron.

I whistled. "Exactly."

Sophia cringed. "There is another, somewhat worse scenario. A possibility exists that should she die, whatever entity is powering this ritual would be free to enter this world without limitation. Not even the vampires want that to happen."

Aaron, Crystal, and I exchanged an 'oh shit' glance.

"Shoot. That doesn't make sense either," said Crystal, tapping her lip. "They planned to make her into a vampire when she turned eighteen, and killing is a required part of that process. If murdering her would blow up their ritual, they couldn't have made her into a vampire."

"She wouldn't have been the only remaining Wakefield in that case," said Sophia.

"Merely the only *living* one left." I frowned.

Sophia nodded. "And changing someone into a vampire is not quite the same as simply killing them."

"Can we all just agree that Blair being hurt is a bad thing?" asked Sophia in a painfully desperate tone.

Choked up, Crystal hugged her. "Yeah."

"Okay, magic debate aside. We're wasting time." I started to walk toward the exit but stopped, realizing I had no idea where to go. "We should be figuring out how to find her."

"Definitely." Aaron folded his arms.

I looked at Sophia. "Have you brushed her hair yet?"

Crystal and her mother gasped at the same time.

"Take me home, now!" Sophia jumped into Crystal's arms like a baby.

Not sure which struck me as more strange, seeing a grown woman leap into another grown woman's arms, or that Crystal didn't struggle at all to support her mother's weight. Still not entirely sure why for Crystal to take someone else with her while teleporting, that person couldn't be in contact with the ground. But magic is weird. Fey magic even more so.

"Mom… are you sure?"

"Do it!"

Crystal flashed a weak smile at me. "Would you mind meeting us back at the house, guys?"

"Sure."

Crystal held her mother close—and the two vanished out of their clothes.

"That's an entirely new level of awkward I'm not prepared to even think about," said Aaron.

I stooped to pick up both handbags and all the clothes on the floor. "So don't think about it. Think about finding Blair. Let's go!"

Chapter Thirteen
Divination

To avoid alerting the deputies, Aaron re-
frained from sending anything out over the
radio about Blair as we rushed back to the
Bradbury estate.

Meanwhile, this was the first time in my life
I'd ridden inside a police vehicle with the lights
and siren on. Apparently, Crystal pre-warned
Pierce we'd be coming. The gate opened for us
before we got close enough to use the intercom.

The butler escorted us to a room on the
second story. Crystal, in a black top, jeans, and
dark boots, paced around behind a small sofa
where Sophia sat, leaning forward over a table
littered with magical paraphernalia. From the

look of things, she'd been so focused on finding Blair, she hadn't bothered 'wasting time' getting dressed. Crystal had wrapped a sheet around her, which made her look like some kind of ancient mystical priestess communing with powers beyond mortal comprehension.

Crystal ran over and hugged me.

"Has Sophia seen anything yet?" I asked.

"No, not yet. Soon, I think. Max, I'm so worried..."

"We'll find her." I squeezed her. "I'm sure we will."

She sniffled. "I just hope she's still alive when we do. Another, even worse, thought hit me."

"Do I want to know?"

"What if they decided not to wait for her to turn eighteen to curse her?"

I clenched my jaw. "I'm not sure I could bring myself to destroy a child vampire. I really freakin' hope they haven't done that. Besides, we still have at least an hour of daylight left."

Sophia gasped and rolled her head around before saying, "Shadow... Pines..." in a trance-like voice.

"Shh. It's happening, Max," whispered Crystal.

'No kidding' almost came out of my mouth, but I held strong and resisted.

"Trees." Sophia's eyes fluttered and opened. She shook off the haze of the magic. "She's running through the forest. Chased. I see a police truck. She's hurting."

"No…" Crystal ran over and grabbed her mother. "They bit her?"

Sophia shook her head rapidly, making her strawberry blonde hair fly about. "Her wrists. Handcuffs. Too tight."

"But, she's running." I rushed over. "That means she escaped. Where is she?"

"Forest. I can't tell where. All the trees around here look the same to me. I don't think it's far from town."

"If she's close to a department vehicle, we might be able to find them." Aaron held up a cell phone. "All police vehicles have GPS transponders. Sec. Keeping this off the radio." He poked an entry in his contacts and held the phone to his ear.

"Hey, Patty. It's Aaron. Got a sensitive missing child situation that I need to keep off the radio because the kidnappers have stolen one of our trucks. Are you seeing any patrol units moving around outside town?"

A woman's voice murmured from the phone, too indistinct to make out words.

"Right. Uh huh. Hook Pond? Yeah, Larson's place was broken into. No, we didn't find his remains. But the kidnappers could've stolen the truck from his driveway. You're a lifesaver, Pat. Thanks." Aaron lowered the phone. "She sees one of our units out by Hook Pond."

"Larson?" Sophia sat up out of her slouch. "One of the deputies who told us Social Services wanted to talk to her was named that."

"They took her out in the middle of nowhere?" Crystal shivered. "That's not good."

We all stared at each other in silence, sharing a moment of mutual horror at the idea they meant to kill her. Either our assumption of what happens to the ritual if Blair dies is wrong, or these vampires are clueless. Possible, since we cleaned out the whole Wakefield clan. Other bloodsuckers might not know what's in the basement—or maybe they do. That could be a big ass problem.

"Why are we just standing here?" Crystal hurried to the chair where I'd dumped the clothes and handbags. I'd have made a joke about a woman refusing to go anywhere without her purse, but Crystal's bag held plenty of hardware she'd no doubt need—like her magical sword. She ran out into the hall so fast she nearly flattened Darth Grandmother. Maybe the old one didn't quite deserve that nickname anymore, but she did insist on constantly wearing dark dresses that made her look like she attended a funeral—in 1930.

I managed to stop before knocking the old one over.

"What's going on?" asked the elder.

"Blair's been kidnapped by mind-controlled sheriff's deputies working for the vampires. We're going after her."

I expected a 'just what are you supposed to do about it' smirk, but she merely nodded once.

Sophia emerged from the sitting room. Between wearing a bed sheet for a dress, frazzled hair, and reddened eyes, she looked like a refugee from a destroyed medieval village or a crazed witch from some fantasy movie.

"Come, dear…" Grandmother escorted her back into the sitting room. "It'll be all right."

Okay, more than vampires, seeing that old woman show empathy was messed up. I guess she *did* have emotions other than bitterness. Dammit. Now I'm thinking of her as a human being. Depression takes a lot of different forms. Ever since her son Sterling died, she's been—as Crystal says—impossible. Well, I suppose if I have a chance to rid Shadow Pines of vampires, maybe I can change my opinion of Anna Bradbury.

I sprinted after Aaron, who shouted in alarm at finding Crystal in the driver's seat of his police Tahoe, already driving toward the gate.

As soon as we dashed off the porch, she stopped the truck and climbed into the back seat.

We ran over and jumped in.

"I was just turning it around," said Crystal. "You know, to save time."

Aaron grumbled, clearly not cool with someone driving his cruiser. No one said a word for the almost fifteen-minute ride out of town into the forest. We swerved along a mostly one lane dirt-and-gravel road that occasionally had wider spots where opposing traffic could pass without one car needing to go halfway into the forest. The directions Aaron got from Patty over the phone must have clicked, since he didn't hesitate or appear the least bit confused as to where to go.

A sedan shot out from behind the trees on a curve up ahead, coming toward us with barely enough time for him to dodge. We went halfway off the road—as did the car. If not for the height difference between the Tahoe and the car, the side mirrors would've smashed toge-ther. Aaron ignored the near miss and powered on. A few minutes later, he swerved to the right at a fork onto an even smaller dirt road that seemed more like a trail intended for hikers than anything a vehicle should be driving on. He punched the button for four-wheel drive.

Aaron shut off the flashing bar lights. This

area had such thick forest not even a vampire could've seen us coming from more than fifty feet away... but better safe than heartbroken. Finding Blair dead probably would've made me finish off that bottle of Jack, but it would have ruined Crystal and done far worse to her mother, Sophia.

I also didn't like how fast the sun wanted to disappear. At the Bradbury estate, we'd guessed an hour or so of daylight remained, but that appeared incorrect. Looking at the sky now, I gave us about twenty minutes tops. Shadow Pines felt like a hornet's nest with a time-release plug in the hole. I'd gone and walloped it a few times with a stick and the pissed-off wasps couldn't get out yet. But once that door opened, we needed to be ready—or really far away.

Lush greenery passed on all sides, momentarily filling me with a sense of peace. All my life, being out in the woods had, not to sound too new-age, centered me. That feeling had become many times more intense now, no doubt due to my connection with the elements.

At the bottom of a steep hill on our right, Whitman's Creek bounced over rocks. Calling it a 'creek' made it sound small, but it wasn't. It varied from twenty yards across to almost forty in spots, though the deepest part of it only came up to a man's shoulders. Of course, much of it had such a stiff current it would be a real task to stand still. Tourists loved it for kayaking.

After a short—but supremely bumpy—ride, the terrain leveled off. Aaron slowed to a stop. I peeled my gaze off the river at the bottom of the hill, looked out the windshield, and squeezed the seat. Another sheriff's department Tahoe sat in front of us at the end of a trampled path it had cleared in the vegetation. Both front doors and the left rear door were wide open.

Aaron cut the engine, and we got out.

The forest's quiet usually comforted me, but at the moment, the stillness had the opposite effect, chilling me.

Crystal walked past the truck toward the trees.

Aaron poked his head inside. "Yeah. This is Larson's unit."

"Psst!" whispered Crystal.

I looked over at her.

She waved for us to follow, then prowled into the woods. Having no better ideas, I hurried after her. Aaron hesitated a few seconds, but decided to follow—after taking the shotgun from Larson's truck.

"Where ya going?" asked Aaron.

"Shh," whispered Crystal. "I can smell them."

"Smell them?" Aaron glanced at her. "Vampires?"

Crystal shook her head. "Normal people have recognizable scents, too. The same thing dogs follow."

"And you can pick it up somehow?" Aaron regarded her with an expression of disbelief.

I suppressed a chuckle. "You've seen her teleport and you're skeptical of her sense of smell?"

"Fair point. She missed her calling. Should've been a cop."

Crystal covered her mouth to hold in laughter.

"She's quite a bit too free-spirited for that." I ducked a low-hanging branch.

"Here." Crystal stooped to pick up a small, pink shoe... what she called a 'flat.' "We just got her these this morning." She pocketed it and kept going.

"Son of a bitch," whispered Aaron, gripping his shotgun tight for a second.

"Like I said... she's good."

"I'm a believer."

A few minutes later, voices came from the woods up ahead. The three of us froze in our tracks, listening.

"We'd be back in town by now if not for you," said a man who sounded an awful lot like

Deputy Don Larson, a guy I'd known in passing for years. "Why'd I let you talk me out of putting leg irons on the kid?"

"Because it's cruel," replied another guy with a mild Spanish accent. That had to be Ramirez.

"Cruel?" Don scoffed. "You know what's cruel? Kicking me in the balls. If you hadn't been such a softie, we'd be back in town by now having a beer. We need to kill her, Paul. Who cares if chaining her ankles together is mean?"

Crystal clenched her hands into fists.

Aaron closed his eyes, muttering to himself.

I tapped him on the arm. When he looked at me, I whispered, "We don't have to kill them. Just destroy the vampire controlling them, and the suggestive effect ends."

He nodded. "Good to know."

Silent and careful, we headed in the direction from which the voices came and soon discovered a shallow grave sized for a kid Blair's height. The sight of it made Crystal snarl. Fortunately, the hole was empty and no blood had been spilled here. A collapsible Army shovel lay on the ground next to the hole.

Aaron approached the almost-grave, head bowed. "What the ever-loving hell is going on? They were going to murder a child and friggin' bury her?"

"Not them. Vampires." I pulled on his arm, moving to follow Crystal who'd stormed into the woods. Unlike him, she didn't appear to have any particular problem killing mind-controlled deputies to protect Blair.

Aaron followed, his expression forlorn as if he expected the day would end with him being forced to shoot two more cops.

Larson and Ramirez continuing to bitch at each other over the relative cruelty of putting a second set of handcuffs on the ankles of a ten-year-old they planned to murder was the most surreal conversation I'd ever eavesdropped on. Don Larson, who in no way sounded like a man who'd recently lost his wife, spoke as if Blair punting him in the groin constituted a far worse crime than what they wanted to do to her. Ramirez argued that handcuffing a kid they intended to kill was unnecessarily cruel. Of course, he also sounded surprised that the child had run away, suggesting he'd expected her to just lay there and let them shoot her.

Crystal abruptly veered off to the left, moving away from the deputies who sounded fairly close and a bit to our right. She stopped short at the top of the long, steep hill down to Whitman Creek. After a quick glance back to make sure we'd followed her, she proceeded to make her way down, grabbing trees for balance. I had plenty of hiking experience under my belt, so going down a hill this steep and overgrown didn't faze me too much. What Crystal lacked in hiking experience, she made up for by being agile. Aaron had a little trouble coping with the grade, but he sacrificed speed for stability, avoiding a loud fall that would have alerted the other deputies of our presence.

We climbed down to a fairly narrow strip of flat ground between the hill and the riverbank. Blair's footprints in the dirt, one bare foot, one shoe, headed to the left. Crystal started after her despite Aaron still being halfway up the slope. He could clearly see us, so I didn't wait for him either. He jogged to catch up once he got to the bottom.

"What are we going to do about Larson and Ramirez?" whispered Aaron. "I can't just shoot them."

"I'm sure if it came down to it, you could. But, like I said, we don't have to if we can avoid them now. Destroy the vampire, they go back to normal."

He sighed. "I can't believe they really want to kill that girl."

"*They* don't want to kill her. The vampire is forcing them to. They're not themselves. Stay quiet or they're going to hear us. If we find her before they find us, we don't even need to worry about them."

"All right."

We followed the path of Whitman's Creek for a few minutes.

My cell phone started ringing with the tone that meant a forwarded call from my office number.

"Crap!" I rasped, yanking the thing off my belt clip and mashing the mute button.

The caller ID read 'Morgan, Shiloh.' I didn't recognize the name, even though it struck me as somewhat familiar. Maybe I'd met her in town once. Couldn't be one of Justine's relatives because she didn't have any. Besides, anyone who knew me would've called my cell phone directly, not the office number. A forwarded call meant someone dialed the phone number I published in my PI ads.

My hands were a little full for me to take on a new client at the moment, so I let it drop into voicemail.

A few seconds later, it began vibrating again.

"Dammit."

Chapter Fourteen
Persistent

Despite being on mute, the buzzing of my ringing cell phone was loud enough for Crystal to notice. She looked back at me with an expression like an unanswered phone constituted a mortal offense.

"What?" I whispered.

"You're not going to pick up?"

"There's a little too much going on right now to take on a new client. Plus those two probably heard the ringer. Keep moving."

She resumed walking. "It could be important. What if it's that blogger Michael who's been helping you figure out the elemental stuff? Maybe he found something important."

"He wouldn't call the public line. That ringtone meant someone found one of my flyers or newspaper ads."

The phone stopped ringing, and once again, resumed buzzing after mere seconds.

"At least tell them you'll call them back," said Crystal.

"Persistent, aren't they?" whispered Aaron.

The fourth time it vibrated, I nearly threw it into the forest, but decided to answer. "Max Long." But my mental voice added, 'have you ever heard of voicemail?'

"Mr. Long!" said Blair. "I need help! Two fake cops kidnapped me and tried to kill me! I got away, but I don't know where I am."

Crystal whirled to face me, her eyes huge. Damn, she's got good ears.

"Where are you?" I asked.

"Umm. Some giant old ruined house in the middle of the forest. It's really creepy here, but not as bad as where you found me."

Holy cow… come to think of it, we were close to Shadow Pines Manor, that abandoned boarding house. It occurred to me that earlier, while in a trance, Sophia had said 'Shadow Pines.' But could she have meant this house before Blair even got here? Maybe.

"I know the place," I said, gripping my phone far harder than necessary. "We're already close. Be careful, there might be vampires in there."

"Okay." The girl made an uneasy noise. "I can't get out of these handcuffs. After I got away the first time, they put like a cord around my waist. I'm like seriously stuck."

"It doesn't matter. You don't have to fight vampires. Just find a hiding place. We'll be right there."

"But I can't reach doorknobs! And crap, this phone's about to die!"

"Oh, hey guys," said Aaron from behind me. "What's up?"

Shit.

I glanced over my shoulder at Don Larson and Paul Ramirez walking up to us. Neither one of them looked at all normal. In fact, they had the same 'serial killer' glint in their eyes Chuck did right before he pulled a gun. That probably happened as soon as they saw me.

"Be there soon." I spun toward the deputies, raising my left hand in a gesture that bent the wind to my desire.

Don and Paul both went for their guns, but didn't get them all the way out of their holsters before the hurricane-force air blast hurled them off their feet.

Aaron pointed the shotgun at them and shouted, "Toss the weapons!"

Knowing the deputies wouldn't listen to him, I beckoned to the earth, hollowing out a pit beneath the two men. Ten feet deep should hold them. Their complete lack of shouting, threatening, or making much noise at all confirmed they'd gone full thrall, little more than machines at this point.

"I know where she is!" I shouted above the already dying wind. "That was Blair on the phone."

Crystal grabbed my arm. "Yeah. Heard her. Where the heck is she?"

"I'll tell you when we're out of earshot of those two," I said, pointing to the pit of deputies. I took her hand and ran along the creek, vaguely remembering something about a foot trail running up the hill between the water and the boarding house property so residents could go fishing or swimming. Then I remembered I still had her on the line. "Blair?" I asked into the phone.

But the line had dropped. Dammit.

I stuffed the phone back in its holder, released Crystal's hand, and ran even faster. Aaron pounded somewhere behind.

Chapter Fifteen
Little Help

A quarter mile from where we left the deputies stuck in a hole, I found a small wooden pier that probably would've collapsed under the weight of a fat squirrel.

A decaying folding chair still sat at the end, possibly holding the ghost of a former boarding house resident who liked to fish. I looked away from the pier to the left, tracing a straight line with my gaze to a heavily overgrown trail that led up the hill.

Squarish logs formed 'steps' at regular intervals, though in my opinion, they did nothing to make the trail easier to follow. As fast as the treacherous, winding path allowed, we hurried through a series of back and forth switchbacks on a steep uphill grade. At the top, we emerged next to century-disused outhouses at the end of the long, open parking area—basically an over-grown dirt lot—in front of the old boarding house.

The Shadow Pines Manor hadn't been officially open for decades. Though it rivaled any of the Founding Families' estates for size, the three-story structure definitely showed its abandonment. Unsurprisingly, no one had re-paired the boards I'd blasted off the windows while fighting Derek and Piper. Justine hadn't even bothered to put crime scene tape on the porch.

We had minutes of daylight left.

I ran across the grass-covered dirt parking lot in front of the place, and up onto the porch. A small mud print confirmed Blair had kicked the door open already. I pushed past it into the foyer, unsure if the smell of death in the air still lingered from Piper and Derek or if this place had new tenants. Aaron and Crystal barreled in behind me.

Dust coated the dark brown wood of the parlor on my right. Blair's footprints, clearly hers due to having only one shoe on, approach-ed the parlor but didn't go past the arch, veering back to the carpeted area by us. The rug didn't have enough dust for her to leave tracks. She could've gone straight, deeper into the house, or upstairs.

The urge to call out for her almost made me yell, but I decided not to risk alerting any fiends in the house, or the deputies if they'd managed to climb out of that pit and come after us.

"I'll check the third floor," I said. "Crystal, second, Aaron, ground?"

They both nodded grimly.

Crystal and I started toward the stairs while Aaron headed into the hallway—until Blair's shriek came from upstairs, which sent all three of us barreling up toward the continued screaming coming from the third floor.

Three flights up, I rushed off the top of the stairs and into the hallway. Considering she'd clearly been discovered and silence blown, I shouted, "Blair?"

Crystal and Aaron skidded to a stop on either side of me.

"Blair!?" yelled Crystal.

The thumping of a child running on old wooden floor came from my left. I took one step in that direction, but stopped short when Blair scrambled around the corner at the far end of the hall. The rug tore out from under her feet as she tried to negotiate the turn, throwing her into the wall chest-first since her hands were locked behind her back. Amazingly, she bounced off the wall, kept her balance, and resumed running for us.

"Help!" screamed Blair. "It's right behind me!"

Expecting a vampire to be chasing her, I held my ground and raised my arm. A thirtyish man with glowing red eyes rounded the corner —right into my lightning bolt. The concussive *boom* of the powerful electrical discharge flung Blair into a stagger, knocked dust off the walls, broke the window at the end of the hallway, and deafened me for a few seconds.

The vampire, however, got the worst end of the deal, exploding into a cloud of smoldering ashes.

Blair crashed into me, sobbing, struggling furiously at the handcuffs. She clearly wanted to wrap her arms around me and cling. I didn't enjoy seeing her this upset and terrified, but at least it proved her a normal kid.

I put an arm around her and squeezed, hoping a firm hug would comfort her since she couldn't cling to me. "Hey, kid, you okay?"

She swallowed a sob. "Mostly. Not hurt, just freaked out big time."

"How the heck did you call us?" Crystal tapped the cuffs to magically unlock them, then sprouted one claw from her index finger to cut the giant plastic zip tie around her waist.

Blair clamped her arms around me, trembling. "Someone left a touch screen cell phone in one of the bedrooms. Dialed with my nose, but it didn't have much power. The battery died in the middle of the call."

"Oh, that's why the name sounded familiar. Shiloh… one of those college kids we found here." I patted Blair on the head. "We got you. You're okay now."

She squirmed to include Crystal in the group hug. "They were gonna kill me. Tried to shoot me when I ran away. I fell down a hill and hid inside a hollow tree. They didn't see me and kept going." She sniffled, swallowed hard. "Why are fake cops trying to *kill* me? What did I do?"

"It's not your fault," said Crystal.

"Absolutely not." I grumbled. "They're not fake cops, they're mind-controlled actual cops."

Still shivering, Blair tried to say something but ended up crying for almost a full minute before she regained the ability to speak. "I was hiding in a bedroom. Then that guy climbed out of a hole in the floor. He looked at me and his eyes started to glow. Jerk said 'who ordered delivery' and tried to grab me. I heard more of them moving in the hole."

A door slammed somewhere downstairs.

"Time to go," said Aaron. "The sun's about done setting."

"What's going on? Why are they trying to kill me? I'm just a kid."

I sighed. "Probably because you're likely a key to stopping all the vampires."

"*All* of them?" She gawked at me.

"Well, no… only the ones in Shadow Pines."

"Oh, so nothing serious then." She shivered, her frightened facial expression not at all matching her blasé tone of voice.

"Here." Crystal fished the stray shoe out of her bag. "You lost this in the woods."

Blair didn't seem able to make herself let go of us, so Crystal put it on for her.

"If anyone makes a Cinderella joke, I will punch them." Blair sniffle-laughed.

Don Larson and Paul Ramirez slow-walked up the stairs, glaring at me. They didn't at all look happy. Probably had something to do with me dropping them into a giant hole. I knew I should've covered it with a stone slab. Nah, they would've suffocated.

Another man appeared at the corner Blair had run out from, his eyes glowing red so bright they looked like laser pointers. Shit. Vampire—likely multiple vampires—in front of us; two mind-controlled deputies behind us on the stairs. This isn't going to end well.

"Not gonna dig a freakin' hole in here, asshole." Larson glared at me—and went for his gun.

Chapter Sixteen
Unruly Guests

"Don't!" shouted Aaron, aiming his shotgun at the deputies.

Blair screamed, gesturing frantically at the vampire coming down the hall.

Crystal did the most logical thing possible when confronted by a pair of possessed sheriff's deputies trying to murder us... deputies we didn't want to kill: she lifted her shirt and gave them a good look at her red lace bra.

Both men's expressions melted from soulless automaton to dumbfounded grin.

Meanwhile, Aaron swung around and pumped two shells into the vampire running at us. The fiend largely ignored the hit to the chest, but the second shot took out his left knee and knocked him sliding on his face. Since Crystal offered our best chance at getting out of here without killing innocent deputies, I turned my attention to the vampire and covered him in flames.

No, I didn't forget we basically stood inside a giant pile of tinder and matchsticks. As soon as the vamp ashed over, I commanded the rapidly spreading flames to go out.

"Umm," whispered Blair, staring at Crystal. "What the heck are you doing?"

"I'm charming them… needed to make it work fast."

I ran over to the two dumbstruck deputies and took their handguns, stuffing one in the back of my jeans and tossing the other to Crystal.

While the entranced deputies continued to stare at Crystal, I used the discarded handcuffs to chain them to a radiator pipe along the wall. Just as I snapped the cuffs in place, another vampire flashed up the steps, and two more appeared along the third-floor hallway. The vampire on the stairs leapt over the banister and tackled me into the wall beside the deputies.

A blast from Aaron's shotgun shredded the knee out from under one of the vamps coming down the hall, but I had bigger problems at the moment—fangs in my face. Stair Vampire pinning me against the crumbling wallpaper had the strength of a small truck. No idea if he knew I needed my hands to call on the elements or not, but he pinned my wrists above my head and leaned in to bite me on the neck. Wait, I didn't need my hands for defense.

As soon as I commanded the power of earth into my body, hardening my skin to stone, my abruptly increased weight caused me to break through the floor.

Oops.

My now-thousand-pound-self plummeted, dragging the vampire holding me down by his grip on my wrists. I hit the second story floor like a spear, my feet punching a hole, but ended up stuck at the waist. Above me, a shotgun went off. Screaming, Blair ran down the stairs into view right in front of me.

"Whoa," said the vampire, flat on his chest in the hall between me and the stairs. "The hell is this shit?"

At seeing a vampire still holding my arms, Blair stopped short and clung to the banister bars, her gaze rapidly shifting back and forth from the vampire on me to the mess above her. She looked like a mouse caught between a diving eagle and a lynx.

As soon as the vampire let go of me, I

shoved my right hand into his face and fire-blasted him. He howled, punching me a few times in the head before the flames consumed him into a dusting of dark grey ash. His attack didn't hurt *too* much, but the sheer strength behind the punches left me a bit loopy for a few seconds despite me having an outer layer of stone.

Blair's shrill scream snapped me back to the here and now. She ducked, covering her head with both arms, avoiding a vampire pulling a Superman flight down the stairs. He sailed above her and smashed face-first into the wall on the switchback landing between the second and third story. After he crumpled to the floor, she scrambled down the last few steps and ran to me.

"Missed me," chimed Crystal from the third.

My being stuck waist deep in the floor gave the child a height advantage. She grabbed my arm and tried to pull me out, but didn't accomplish much. Figured I had no chance of pulling myself up in my present state. This stone skin weighed far too much. Even if I had the strength to lift myself, the floor would crumble out from under me. So, I reverted back to flesh and bone... and climbed up to a kneeling position.

The shotgun went off again.

Three vampires bashed down a door to my left, scrambled into the hallway, and started running toward us. The two deputies upstairs struggled to break the radiator pipe, banging and thudding at the wall.

"Uh oh," whispered Blair, backpedaling.

I thrust my arm out, calling lightning. The arc went off with a robust thunderclap. Blair clamped her hands over her ears. A shaft of electricity as thick as my forearm jumped over all three fiends. The one nearest me exploded. The second one fell in two pieces, his body from pectorals to hips having disintegrated. Vampire three more or less survived with a head-sized hole in his chest. He hit the floor screaming in agony.

The vampire who ate wall at the landing glanced briefly at Blair and me, but appeared angrier at Crystal, so he ran upstairs, chasing her. At the *boom* of a shotgun firing, he flew butt-first back down the stairs to the landing. Crystal rushed after him and thrust her sword through his face into the wall. Hissing, he raked his claws at her for a few seconds, but fell limp when she wrenched the blade around in a twist.

I projected a stream of flames into the screaming vampire, silencing him, then finished burning the remains of the one the lightning bolt had torn in half.

Blair stared at the ashes, no readable expression on her face.

"You okay?" I asked.

"I don't like vampires," whispered the child.

"Neither do I. Try not to look at them so you don't have bad dreams."

Aaron thundered down the steps, Crystal right behind her.

"I've already seen worse things in my dreams than this." Blair swatted ash off her sleeves.

I squeezed her shoulder. "You poor kid."

"I'm not poor. I have piles of money." She cracked a bit of a grin. "Don't really care about it though. I'd give it all away to stay alive and have a real family."

A red-haired vampiress popped up out of the hole I'd made in the second floor. The bitch grabbed my left ankle and yanked me off my feet. I fell flat on my chest, the wind knocked out of me.

Blair screamed, mostly from surprise.

Aaron clicked the trigger of the shotgun, but got only a *click*. No boom. Crystal swiped her sword at the woman's wrist. The fiend let go of me and jerked her arm back fast enough to avoid losing her hand. I sat up and projected a flamethrower from my palm right into her face. Shrieking, the vampiress fell out of sight and landed with a *thud* on the first floor. Thumping and agonized shrieking followed.

I jumped up and peered down at the flailing, burning humanoid shape. The instant her body broke apart to ashes, I quelled the fire. Crystal grabbed Blair's hand and pulled her to the stairs, following Aaron down to the first floor. Another pair of vamps kicking their way out of a bedroom behind me delayed me. Whirling, I raised my arms and called two lightning bolts. As the bloodsuckers hit the floor burning, a third vampire emerged from a hole in the ceiling a ways off down the corridor. He, too, enjoyed a sizzling lightning bolt to the face. His head exploded in an instant, the rest of his body bursting into ash so fast nothing solid hit the floor when he fell out of the ceiling.

This place had deteriorated inside to the degree the vamps climbed walls and went through holes in the floors and ceilings. I felt like a human invading a nest of life-sized termites who didn't have to obey the laws of gravity. Shouting and the clanging of blades echoed up from downstairs.

Dammit. We had to get the hell out of here, and the vamps definitely did *not* want to play nice. I ran downstairs to find Aaron wrestling a short, skinny dude dressed like he'd come out of the 1980s. Son of a bitch even had a mullet.

Crystal engaged in a swordfight against a long-haired man in a suit wielding a katana. He had a clear advantage in both skill and speed, forcing her to keep backing away rapidly to avoid being sliced to ribbons.

I tried to draw a bead on him for a lightning bolt, but the two of them kept spinning around each other so fast I didn't trust myself not to hit her, too.

He parried the sword out of her hand so hard she fell flat on her front, defenseless in front of him. An angry shout bellowed out of me as I channeled a lightning bolt. Katana vampire raised his blade to take her head off—but a spear burst out of the back of her jeans and impaled him under the chin, the point bursting out the top of his head.

Stunned by the sight, I hesitated, sparks dancing over my fingers.

Crystal lunged for her sword, grabbing it as she sprang to her feet in a spinning slash that took his head off. What I'd mistaken for a spear was a prehensile tail tipped with an onyx barb—the same barb that had burst out of that other vampire's chest at The Black Rose club. She had an array of various concealed parts. I had a Swiss Army girlfriend. How many attachments *did* she come with?

Aaron howled in pain.

Blair screamed.

I spun to the left. The little mullet vampire had bitten the deputy on the shoulder. Kinda looked like a chihuahua picking a fight with a German shepherd. The vamp hung from his fangs, his feet not reaching the floor. Only my inherent animosity toward vampires kept me from finding the sight hilarious.

"That's a big tick, Aaron," I said, before throwing a smaller stream of fire into the vampire's back. "Hold still a moment while I burn it out."

Shrieking, Mullet Boy let go of Aaron and started running in circles, swatting at the flames spreading down his arms. Crystal intercepted, taking his head with a clean stroke of her sword. The inert body hit the ground and succumbed to the fire. In five seconds, he'd turned into a pile of ashes and singed clothing.

"Jesus…" Aaron grabbed his shoulder. "Am I doomed?"

"No." Crystal hurried over to check him. "No worse than if you'd been stabbed by a couple ice picks. The bite doesn't transmit vampirism."

"To be turned into a vampire, you have to have all your blood drained," said Blair. "Once your heart stops beating, then a vampire forces their blood down your throat. The curse takes over and you wake back up as a monster. The vamp needs to desire that the curse be passed on. It's not going to happen from a fight."

"I don't know what bothers me more. That a freakin' vampire just bit me or that a little kid knows all that." Aaron clamped his hand over the wound.

"I watched them make vampires," said Blair.

"Creepy." Aaron glanced at her.

"Not by choice. They forced me to, so I wouldn't be scared when it was my turn. Remington tried to tell me it wouldn't hurt." She looked around, pretending to be worried about eavesdroppers, then whispered, "He lied."

"We have a serious problem," I said.

Everyone looked at me.

"We're still inside this house."

"Not funny." Crystal took Blair's hand again.

"Wasn't trying to be."

Aaron grunted and pushed off the wall. "Then let's go."

I jogged across the foyer, Crystal behind me leading Blair, Aaron bringing up the rear. Upon reaching the outside porch, I stopped short at the sight of a silver BMW that hadn't been there before.

Blair emitted a half-second scream before it muffled like a hand went over her mouth. I spun around as a well-dressed man swept the child off her feet and made to run for the porch railing. Crystal pounced on his back while I grabbed his left arm. Aaron stomped in my direction, hammering the butt-end of his shotgun into the face of a second vampire who'd attempted to ambush me with a small machine gun. The strike didn't do a damn thing insofar as knocking the vampire unconscious, but it did throw him over backward. He clenched down on the trigger, bullets perforating the porch ceiling. Aaron descended on the fiend, mashing the butt end of the shotgun repeatedly into his face.

Blair swung her feet up to catch the railing, shoving back against the vampire trying to jump the railing and go for the car. Crystal sprouted claws and raked at the fiend's throat.

Not that her tiny fingernails had any chance whatsoever of beheading a vampire, but the sensation of a slit throat apparently set off an instinctual terror response. The vamp dropped Blair and launched into a flailing fit, trying to get Crystal off him. I let go of his arm and collected the girl, pulling her clear of any accidental slashing.

Crystal gave the vampire a shove that sent him stumbling forward so he draped over the railing. I threw a lightning bolt into his back, holding the electrical discharge on him for a few seconds until his eyeballs exploded and his body caught fire.

"Dammit!" I rasped, "How many vampires *are* there in this town?"

"How many people have gone missing around here?" asked Crystal.

"Ugh." I groaned. "That's a big number."

Blair squeezed me around the waist so hard I expected the burger I ate hours ago to come flying back out.

"Shh. It's okay. I think that's the last of them here anyway… and these two looked more interested in abducting you than killing you."

"That's not making me feel better," whispered Blair. "The last time someone kidnapped me, they wanted to kill me, just way off in the forest."

"We're already way off in the forest," I said, trying to pat her head comfortingly. "These two wanted something else, but what?"

Crystal searched their wallets and also found a pair of cell phones in the ash piles. "Phones are locked, and I'm sure these IDs are fake."

Aaron moved to the end of the porch, grabbing his shoulder mic. "Tim, this is Wilson, copy?"

"Tim didn't show up," replied Patty. "I'm still freakin' here. Still the only one in the damn building. I'm going to sleep on my desk tonight, I bet. I've had to send a handful of issues over to the state police. You better be telling me you're working a double tonight, too."

"I've been awake so long I forgot what sleep is like. I'm not near the truck right now. Can you run a plate and tell me who owns it?" He read off the license number on the BMW.

The handcuffed Larson screamed in anger, his bellow echoing out from a third-floor window.

Blair shivered in response. "Let's get out of here before they break loose."

"What are we gonna do about those two?" asked Crystal.

"Leave them there for now. We can come back tomorrow morning."

"That tag's registered to Ambrose Farrington," said Patty from the radio.

Crystal narrowed her eyes. "Nigel."

"Isn't he dead?" I asked.

"Supposedly." Aaron thanked Patty for her help then let go of the mic. "The body was badly mauled. Sheriff Waters declared it a bear attack. I suppose it could have been anyone really. Would've needed dental records to iden-tify the body for sure."

"The vampire who killed Nigel wouldn't have been careless," said Crystal.

Blair nudged me toward the steps, away from the house, so I walked with her down onto the grassy parking lot. Crystal and Aaron followed.

"Nigel was an occultist who wanted to steal your soul so he could empower an enchanted object that would give him the power to control the city—or at least control the Founding Families. Is it that hard to imagine that a man capable of doing something like that could trick a vampire into believing he'd been killed? Nigel might not be as dead as we thought."

"I guess we're about to find out." She stashed her sword in her purse. "Can we please get her out of here before more vampires show up?"

"I like that idea," said Blair.

"The truck is about a third of a mile off." Aaron pointed. "More or less that way."

"Rough hike in the dark. Thick underbrush." I patted Blair on the arm. "Let go, hon. Hop on my back if you want. Those shoes aren't great for hiking. They're thinner than tissues."

Aaron, the only one of us with a flashlight, took the lead. I stooped so Blair could climb up like a human backpack. Poor kid still shivered in fear. Couldn't blame her after what happened. Yeah, some therapist is going to milk *two* boats out of her.

Chapter Seventeen
Poop to Fan Contact

The walk to Aaron's Tahoe didn't suck as bad as I expected. Meaning, no vampires bothered us even if it was a hike across overgrown forest in pitch dark. All of us expected a flashlight out here would've drawn vampires from as far away as town, but we got lucky. Blair crawled into the back seat, now clinging to Crystal. I took the front passenger seat.

Aaron flopped behind the wheel, staring out into space. "I can't believe I'm still awake. When this is over—*if* I survive—I'm gonna sleep for an entire day."

"You and me both," I said.

He started the engine, managed a K-turn,

and drove back out of the woods the way we came in. Blair started frantically begging us to go to the police station to let Sophia out of the interview room, but calmed down once she learned we'd already done that. Aaron didn't drive much faster than a person could walk until we got off the oversized hiking path onto the road. Again, calling it a road required a certain generosity of language.

Tingles welled up in my arms and legs without apparent reason. It neither hurt nor bothered me, but it did create a strong sense of urgency. Maybe Mom Nature tried to tell me the vampires would be coming at us hard, or feral crazy. Or both.

"So… what now? Take the kid to the Bradbury estate?" asked Aaron.

"That's the first place they'll look for her. Unless we camp out there for the night and go full defensive to make sure she stays un-kidnapped. Safest place for her is with Crystal and me. And hiding out tonight is not something that feels possible. I'm getting this weird sense that the shit's about to hit the fan in a big way."

"Don't swear in front of her." Crystal prodded the back of my seat.

"My entire family died and turned into vampires who kept me locked up most of my life.

Two possessed cops tried to murder me. I had to watch them dig a grave for me. Do you really think me hearing a bad word is going to do any more damage?"

Heh. "I like this kid."

Aaron looked at her via the rear view mirror. "You didn't run off while they were digging?"

"Tried, but they used plastic handcuffs to tie the metal handcuffs to a tree. I wasn't strong enough to break them. When the old guy cut me loose from the tree after they finished digging, I kicked him in the balls and ran."

I clenched my jaw, thinking about Paul Ramirez. If he hadn't objected to Don wanting to cuff her ankles, that kid would be dead right now. Maybe the domination hadn't been complete with him? I'd like to think some part of Ramirez' true self fought off the compulsion enough to give her the chance to get away. Larson, on the other hand, probably saw his wife die or found her body and gave up fighting.

Why the hell did the Farringtons want to abduct her? Wait, Nigel was—or is—someone who went well beyond 'dabbling' in magic. He might have had something to do with the whole damn ritual. "Crystal? Do you think your mom has figured anything out yet?"

"Oh, crap. I gotta call her and let her know

Blair's okay." Crystal took out her phone.

"Let's head out to the Farrington manor," I said to Aaron.

Aaron glanced at me. "Didn't they just try to kidnap her? Isn't it stupid to bring her right to them? We kill the vampires who tried to kidnap her and bring her to that place, only to bring her there ourselves?"

"Potentially. But I don't trust leaving her somewhere that I'm not, and Nigel Farrington would never expect it. We know that their family is eyeball deep in vampires. Maybe not to the same degree as the Wakefields were, but I can say with a hundred percent certainty there will be vamps at the place. The more of them we destroy, the better for Shadow Pines. Also, the Bradbury family has had dealings with vampires. A bloodsucker could go there under false pretenses, trick Grandmother, and attack Blair before anyone realizes their true motivation."

Blair gasped, shivering. "Vampires go there?"

Crystal came up for air from her phone conversation long enough to say, "Not anymore. Mother is trying to convince Grandmother it's too dangerous to be involved with them." Crystal, Blair, and Sophia had an emotional conversation via phone for a few minutes.

Aaron handed me the shotgun and pointed at the glove compartment. "Mind reloading that, please? I'm busy driving."

"Mother is still interpreting the pictures. She needs a little more time, but at least she can concentrate on it now that she knows we found Blair." Crystal pulled the child into a hug. "Most of the families had arrangements with vampires to do certain tasks in exchange for money, favors, or influence. Kind of like how even the nicest noble families in the old world sometimes hired assassins—because everyone else had them."

"That's a stupid reason," said Blair. "They're bad. Once the curse sets in, vampires aren't the people they look like anymore. They're monsters. All of them need to burn."

"I'm with the kid." I paused reloading to hold a finger up. "We're going to the Farrington Manor."

"What?" Blurted Crystal and Blair at the same time.

Chapter Eighteen
Back from the Dead

By the time we arrived at the Farrington's estate, another massive property a few miles outside Shadow Pines, I'd managed to convince Crystal and Blair that going there wasn't the single most bone-headed idea of my life. Nature had given me a powerful weapon against vampires, the best we had unless we found a literal flamethrower or machine gun loaded with silver bullets.

Better the kid stay close to us even if that meant bringing her to a place full of vampires. After all, they'd be coming after us—and Blair —regardless of where we went. If we went to them, at least I'd know which direction they'd be coming from and when.

Surprisingly, this manor didn't have a mot-orized gate blocking off the front courtyard, so we rolled right in and parked near the front entrance. Two men in black suits stood like guards by the door. They looked a bit too pale to be alive. I opened the passenger side door and stepped out. Both security vampires glared at me.

The one on the left stepped forward. "This is private prop—"

I hurled two lightning bolts, one from each hand, at the same time, striking the vampires each in the chest. The shock flung them against the wall. They bounced off, collapsing to the porch and smoking, but didn't stop moving. A second bolt ashed them.

"Not in the mood to talk, eh?" asked Aaron.

"Nope." I walked up to the door. "Not to vampires."

Aaron and Crystal got out of the Tahoe and ran up behind me. Blair followed.

Crystal stared at her. "What are you doing, young lady?"

"No way am I staying in the truck. Someone will grab me while you're in there."

"Lock the doors," said Crystal.

"And a vampire won't just punch the win-dow in?" Blair shook her head.

"Fine… Just, stay back." Crystal slipped past me and tapped the lock on the front door, opening it.

A thin older man in a butler's suit approached, walking beside a long-haired man in his forties wearing a nicer suit. He didn't look beefy at all, but vampires didn't have to be. The reek of bog corpse rolled off the thin man. The butler only stank like overpriced cologne.

"I do hope you have a warrant," said the butler, mostly to Aaron. "Or I'm afraid I need to ask you to leave."

I casually raised my hand in a 'get a load of this guy' kind of way, then poured fire all over the vampire standing beside the butler. The fiend collapsed, screaming for three seconds before his body disintegrated. "That's the only warrant I have. I can show it to you if you like."

Crystal widened her eyes at me.

"Ahem." The butler leaned back. "That won't be necessary… what's the meaning of this?"

I glanced at Crystal, pointing my thumb at the butler. "That's the first time I've ever had someone sincerely say 'what's the meaning of this' at me. Is that worth a quarter in the cliché jar?"

"Yeah, I think so. You're, umm, not going to seriously burn living humans, are you?"

"No. Well, not unless they come after us with a lethal weapon." I looked back at the butler. "Where's Nigel? We know he's not dead." We technically didn't know that for a fact, but nothing better than blind confidence to prop up a lie. Say something with total conviction, and some people will question what they know to be true.

The butler stammered at me, unable to think of what to say.

Three vampires, two women and a man, all in their early twenties, rushed out of an interior hallway. I really hated attacking women, but told myself that they stopped being women when they died, merely fiends with pretty outsides. Snarling, I threw a lightning bolt that arced across all of them. The shortest woman burst into a cloud of ash. The other two lapsed into a jittery convulsive fit. Crystal rushed forward, yanking her sword out of her purse, beheading both twitching fiends while Aaron kept his shotgun trained on the butler.

I strolled over and flamethrowered the headless remains.

"W-what are you doing?" the butler gawked at me. "You can't just… just…"

"Shadow Pines is done being a playground for the undead." I faced him, raising my hands to either side and calling a fierce wind to push him out of our way against the wall. Two vases fell, a painting went flying like a giant ninja star, and something I didn't see off to the right smashed like porcelain. "Where's Nigel?"

"This way, if you would follow me."

Crystal blinked. Her expression said 'holy shit, Nigel's really alive?'

The shaking old man led us down the hallway, passing several wide wooden arches. I didn't trust him as far as Blair could judo throw a sumo wrestler, but if he brought us to a room full of vampires, it would only save me the trouble of hunting them down.

"In here." The butler stopped at a set of ornate double doors, fairly deep in the core of the house. He glanced at me briefly, then turned back to open them... revealing a big library.

Straight ahead, a wide carpet ran under two huge tables littered with books. Tall shelves filled the room on both sides. Models of Da Vinci helicopters, moving sculptures of planetary orbits in bronze, and a pterodactyl hung from the ceiling on wires. Past the two tables, a slightly raised portion of wooden decking surrounded by a brass banister held multiple desks. A sixtyish grey-haired man in a nice suit sat at one such desk, deeply engrossed in a huge book.

"You first." I gestured at the butler to go in.

He emitted a nervous sigh, but obliged, entering the room and calling out, "Master Farrington. You have guests."

We followed him inside.

Nigel Farrington glanced over at us, realized who'd come calling, and flashed a broad smile. He stood, mumbling under his breath. One of the rings on his left hand emitted a bright pink-purple glow. The same light shot forth like lasers from Crystal's eyes. Her grip on the sword failed and the weapon clattered to the floor.

"Kevin, would you kindly render these two unconscious?" asked Nigel in a blasé tone, as if requesting more tea. "Crystal, bring the child to me."

"Crap," I said, emitting a bit of a sigh.

Crystal grabbed Blair, scooped her off her feet, and ran deeper into the library, heading for the far left corner. A huge, muscular dude who'd been standing near the wall by the door behind us rushed Aaron, grabbing the shotgun before he could aim it at the giant security guy.

Screw it. I raised my hand at Nigel—and the lightning I tried to call didn't happen. I stared at my hand and tried again.

Nigel chuckled. "Ahh, Mr. Long. I'm afraid your parlor tricks don't work in here. The library is warded. Only *I* can use the art in here."

"Let the child go." I walked around the nearest large table and stalked toward him. "You want me out of your way? Here I am. Let the kid go and release Crystal."

Kevin picked Aaron up and slammed him on the floor.

"Oof!" barked Aaron. "Son of a bitch…"

"What makes you think I intend to harm the child?" asked Nigel. "If she dies, the spell we worked so hard to create breaks."

"Bullshit." I narrowed my eyes. "The vamps have been trying to kill her."

Aaron jumped upright, drawing his baton and hammering Kevin in the gut twice—before the big man palmed the deputy's face and threw him to the floor again.

A door in the back slammed. Blair, her voice echoing, screamed, "Stop!"

Nigel's eyes twitched. Hmm. Distracted. He must be inside Crystal's mind like using a remote controlled android with camera eyes. "You really do not understand politics, do you, Mr. Long?"

"You got me there. I think politics is more bullshit than anything. Never bothered to pay any attention to it."

He chuckled. "Alas, that it may be, but it is a necessary tool. Other vampires—those not part of the Shadow Pines ecosystem—are attempting to kill the poor girl to weaken the vampires here. If she dies, our power is gone. You must understand it is not in our interest that she comes to harm."

"*Our* power? But you're not a vampire."

Aaron tackled Kevin, hooking his leg in a jiu-jitsu takedown. Despite the security man being bodybuilder huge, the fight surprisingly didn't appear too one-sided at this point. I probably should be helping him, but turning my back on Nigel would be a huge mistake. Plus, the deputy was holding his own, thanks largely to Kevin *not* being a vampire.

Nigel laughed. "Of course not. Not yet anyway. However, I do control them. All the vampires in Shadow Pines are my, for lack of a less insulting term, minions."

"You performed the ritual in the Wakefield basement." I pointed at him.

Grunting and groaning came from Kevin and Aaron.

"I am disappointed, Mr. Long. For a private investigator, you really lack information. Several of the Old Family patriarchs participated in the ritual, but only Edison and myself possessed any true talent with the occult. Now, if you will excuse me... I must say the magic you discovered is something I desperately wished to study, but you have become too much of a liability. For what it's worth, I do thank you for bringing me my succubus, but I cannot let you live." He opened his suit jacket. Like pulling out a gentleman's hip flask, he plucked a small handgun from the inner pocket.

I lifted my hands in the gesture to summon the wind, but nothing happened.

Nigel sighed. "Your magic won't work in here, fool."

The fake disappointed look on my face made him smile.

As he casually raised his arm to aim at me, I reached behind my back, yanked Don Larson's Sig 9mm out from my belt, and emptied half the magazine into Nigel's chest. Rapid gunshots and muzzle flashes filled the cavernous library. The soft *plink* of empty brass bounced off the marble floor. Two orange flashes came from his little gun, but the bullets didn't come anywhere near me.

I'd never seen a more surprised expression on a dead man.

"My magic might not work in here"—I held the gun up a little higher—"but this will."

Just in case he had a vest on, I shot him one more time in the forehead.

Nigel shuddered, and fell over backward.

Chapter Nineteen
High Time for a Break

I spun. Kevin sat on top of Aaron, choking him out, so I aimed at the big guy's head. "Aaron, you're the cop. Am I legally allowed to shoot this guy now?"

Aaron gurgled.

Kevin glanced at me.

"Hi. Yes, this is a real gun. Ask Nigel. Please stop strangling the sheriff's deputy. Pretty sure that's against the law."

The huge guy leaned back a little so he could peer past me. He raised one eyebrow upon noticing Farrington dead. Aaron walloped him with a right cross that knocked him to the side.

Where's Crystal and the kid?" gasped Aaron, sitting up.

"Not sure. You got that guy?" I picked up Crystal's sword.

Kevin raised his hands in surrender.

"I don't have time to deal with you." Aaron pointed at him. "Get the hell out of here and find a new job."

"You're letting him go?" I blinked.

"I should arrest him, but we don't have the resources to process anyone right now. And I don't have the first damn clue how to write up 'assisting an occultist with vampire summoning.'" Aaron shooed the security man. "If you come at me again tonight, I'm just gonna freakin' shoot you. But I'm serious, get out of here, don't cause any more trouble, and I'll forget you tried to kick my ass. I'll also assume you were under some sort of mind control."

Grunting, Kevin rose to his feet and hurried for the exit. Meanwhile, the butler appeared to have vanished into thin air.

I approached Nigel's body and crouched to search him, pocketing the ring he'd used to take control of my girlfriend. If I hadn't seen him use it, I wouldn't have thought it anything unusual, merely gaudy due to its size. He didn't have anything else on him that seemed important to the vampire situation, so I ran for the door Crystal went through, Aaron jogging after me. The hallway on the other side looked like more 'rich person house.' More or less the same in both directions. No carpet or much fabric, so sound in here echoed.

"Crystal?" I shouted. "Blair?"

A faint voice came from the right. Probably Blair yelling 'here.'

We hurried in that direction, as Blair's shouting led us down one more hallway to the kitchen, then a storage room and stairs to the basement. This place held *way* less old furniture than the Wakefield basement—meaning none— being predominantly full of wine racks. However, the back corner had four prison-cell-sized cages made from an enormous mass of bars divided into four chambers.

Crystal stood frozen like a statue, one foot in the leftmost cell, staring forward while holding her arms in a way that suggested she still carried Blair. The girl, meanwhile, was shouting at her to 'snap out of it.' Upon noticing us emerge from the stairwell, Blair ran over and grabbed me.

"You okay?" I asked, patting her on the back.

"Yeah. Crystal was about to stuff me in a cell, but then she went all derpy."

"Does every giant manor house have dungeon cells in the basement?" I shook my head. "No, this has to be something uniquely creepy about Shadow Pines."

"You know rich people and their eccentricities." Aaron whistled.

I gave him side eye.

"Dammit!" roared Crystal.

The three of us jumped at the sudden noise, Blair yelping.

"Argh!" Crystal stormed over to us. "I *hate* being controlled."

"You dropped this." I held out her sword.

She ignored me for the moment, kneeling to grasp Blair's hands in both of hers. "I'm really sorry for taking off with you like that." Crystal blinked. "You're not scared of me..."

"Nope. Wasn't your fault. I know the crazy old guy did something to you."

Smiling, Crystal stood and took her sword from me. "Speaking of crazy old guy. What happened?"

"He's no longer anyone's problem."

"Good," said Crystal. "So what was his deal?"

I hesitated, not really wanting to discuss this in front of the kid, but screw it. She'd seen so much crap already. I gestured at Blair. "Nigel said he didn't want to hurt her. Claimed if she died, it would destroy all the vampires here."

Blair went pale. Well, *paler*. Dracula could look at that girl and say 'damn, kid, you need some sun.'

"Relax." I said to Blair. "I won't let anyone hurt you,"

The child hugged me tight.

To Crystal, I added, "I don't believe Nigel anyway. No way am I going to let anything happen to a kid. Even *if* he wasn't lying, and the easiest way to end the vampire problem in Shadow Pines really *is* killing her, that ain't gonna happen. I'll go down fighting them one at a time before I allow anyone to hurt a child."

Crystal hugged both of us.

"If she believes you, I do too." Blair squeezed me tighter. There might have been a lump in my throat. Maybe.

After a moment, I asked, "But why would Nigel even say that? I mean, he wanted her, which clearly proves she's important somehow."

"Don't make sense." Aaron shook his head. "Vampires forced Don and Paul to try and kill her. They wouldn't do that if it would destroy them all."

Crystal released her grip. "Let's go talk to my mother. Aaron's running on fumes. Blair's had a hell of a day. Maybe holing up at the estate and going on the defensive for the night wouldn't be a bad idea. We can catch a few hours of sleep after sunrise and still have hours left before dark tomorrow."

"Hmm. Not a bad idea. Assuming your home can withstand a vampire assault. And, I hope your grandmother isn't really an elder demon."

She laughed. "Nah. She only acts like it."

"So she's normal?" I raised both eyebrows.

"As normal as a witch gets."

I facepalmed. "Ugh. Didn't you say the magic came from the Darcy side?"

"True, but we're not the *only* ones who practice." She whispered past the back of her hand. "Between you and me, Mother is stronger."

"Heh."

"But…" Crystal took Blair's hand and started for the stairs. "If nothing else, we'll be reasonably safe from vampires on the property. Mother and Grandmother have placed many wards."

I hurled a lightning bolt into the bars of the dungeon cells.

Crystal and Blair both screamed at the sudden *bang*. Aaron winced.

"What was that for?" Crystal gawked at me.

"You said 'wards.' I wanted to make sure Nature still listened to me. It didn't work in the library."

"Wards?" asked Blair, still cringing from the loud blast. "Is that why the vampires sent fake cops to kidnap me?"

"They were real cops, just mind-controlled," I said. "But yes, most likely. If vampires can't get onto the Bradbury estate, they would have needed to use thralls instead."

"Oh… here." I fished the ring out of my pocket and handed it to Crystal.

"What's this?" She eyed it.

"The thing he used to mind control you. I don't want to keep it since it feels all kinds of wrong having a device that could turn my girlfriend into an automaton."

"You say the sweetest things." She batted her eyelashes at me.

"And I don't want anyone else having it. Only option that made sense is giving it to you… or destroying it. Does it do anything useful?"

She examined it. "A mystic's trinket I think. I'd have to ask my mother to double check, but I think the effect of this ring is only making his magic stronger against fey creatures. Nigel used a mind-control spell and this ring amplified it so I couldn't resist."

"So…" I raised an eyebrow. "A normal person wearing that ring wouldn't be able to turn you into a puppet?"

"Nope." She dropped it into her bag. "But I'm also not a hundred percent sure I'm right. Better to keep it out of circulation anyway though."

We headed upstairs, on high alert for additional vampire attacks, but didn't see any—or any humans at all. In fact, not even an irritated micro-dog bothered us on the way outside to the Tahoe.

"You drive," said Aaron, tossing the keys at me. "I'm so beyond done right now."

Chapter Twenty
Focus

On the ride to the Bradbury estate, I thought about Justine.

Not in a missing her romantically sense, just hoping she rested comfortably in a hospital bed and the surgery had gone okay. Shitty of me not to go visit her, but we really did have a good reason. In fact, if she'd been re-controlled, I'm certain she'd have preferred we do this. For all I knew, we'd already destroyed the vampire that might have controlled her, but no sense taking the chance she'd been programmed to kill me. That sort of implanted command wouldn't care about her health. She could kill herself trying to get out of bed to come after me.

We arrived at the manor at 10:49 p.m. according to the dashboard clock. So much had happened today that cooking breakfast for a once-again-mortal Tracy Randall felt further away than fourteen hours ago. I rarely got out of bed as early as I did this morning, which is probably why the day felt as long as two.

Pierce opened the door for us and led us upstairs to a sitting room. Sophia leapt from the sofa she'd been resting on, practically tackling Blair. The child blurting, "Mommy!" brought the woman to tears. Crystal cried, too. And, well, hard-boiled private eyes didn't cry. We got dust in our eyes on occasion, though.

Aaron, too tired to do much of anything else, fell into a wingback chair and closed his eyes.

I didn't fully trust the vampire wards that supposedly protected this house, so my guard remained up. A few minutes later, the emotional storm relaxed enough to allow Sophia to speak. She retreated to her sofa, pulling Blair into her lap. Two days and already clingy. That poor kid is going to have the queen of helicopter moms. But... considering how she'd been largely ignored for her first ten years—and what happened to her today—she's probably not going to mind having an overly attentive mother.

"The ritual done in the Wakefield Manor basement is almost certainly responsible for the massive surge in dark energy within Shadow Pines," said Sophia. "As long as it remains active, the vampires will be a continuous threat here."

"Wait so, vampires only exist because of that ritual?" I raised both eyebrows.

Sophia shook her head. "No. They exist naturally... or unnaturally if you want to be technical. But, rarely would there be more than two or three within a hundred miles of each other. Certainly not dozens, or however many are here. And the ritual magic is making them more powerful."

"How do we stop it?" I asked. "The dark magic, I mean."

Blair tensed.

"Rituals like this utilize various foci. All the materials on that altar are foci. To safely break the ritual, the primary focus needs to be destroyed, but *only* the primary focus. If anything else is damaged, it will become much harder to close the portal."

Crystal blinked. "Portal?"

"What portal?" I raked my hand up through my hair, exhaling hard. "Are they summoning these damn things from, like, hell or something?"

Sophia smiled. "No... not that kind of portal. This is what some refer to as a spirit door. Nothing a person or dark entity can traverse. It is merely a conduit for energy and possibly spirits. You will not be able to see such an opening."

"Ahh." I faked wiping sweat from my brow. "Whew."

"So close this portal and what happens?" asked Crystal. "The vampires disappear? Get weaker? What?"

Sophia bit her lip. "We cannot give you an exact answer to that, only a theory."

"We?" asked Crystal."

"Anna and I."

"Who's Anna?" asked a sleepy Aaron.

Sophia looked over at him with an unreadable expression. "Sterling's mother."

"Darth Grandmother? She's *helping* us?" I feigned having a spell.

"Oh, stop." Crystal poked me. "Anna's not that bad."

I put my hands on my hips. "Okay, yeah maybe you're right. So, what's the idea?"

"Well, Anna and I came up with a theory that whoever created this altar gathered a great amount of energy upon the initial creation of the ritual. When the spell completed, it would have released a surge that most likely affected them, as well as anyone nearby, turning them into vampires."

"They *wanted* to be vampires?" I asked, eyebrows up in total disbelief.

"Doubtful. Likely, they didn't know what would happen. Chances are they merely sought power of some kind. Either an increase in their magical abilities or perhaps extending their life-span. And as you know, it is possible to undo the curse if you destroy the sire before the new vampire has killed."

"Yep." I nodded. "So, in this case, the sire would be he or she who first conducted the ceremony?"

"Yes. And breaking this ritual will destroy any of the original vampires that it created." Sophia squeezed Blair like an oversized teddy bear.

"Oh, wow. So you're saying that all the rest of the vampires will go back to human?" I cringed, starting to regret blowing them up.

"No. I'm afraid not. If they've become permanently cursed, they won't revert to human again... but the source of their vampirism will be gone. They'll turn to dust."

"Well, that saves us the trouble of hunting them down. Sucks they're doomed, but they already were. Saves me the trouble of running around throwing fire everywhere."

"Yeah." Crystal looked down. "It almost sounds possible this town could go back to *not* being a solidified nightmare."

"Oh, I think Shadow Pines will always be… interesting. But, the vampires have truly gotten out of hand." Sophia kissed the back of Blair's head.

Yeah, that kid's in for one clingy mother. Most kids hate overbearing parents, but I think this girl's going to adore it… at least until she's a teenager.

"Right, so which of those things on the table is the primary focus?" I picked up a printout of the photo, examining it. Skull, dagger, bowl of blood with body parts floating in it, candles, papers, cloth bundles that could contain anything. Ugh, I hoped they didn't hold dead animals. Sophia earlier said human sacrifice had been involved. I had the feeling those bundles contained hearts or something nasty. "Is it the skull?"

"We can't tell from looking at a picture." Sophia stroked the girl's hair. "That said, Blair might be able to sense a greater amount of energy in one of the objects than the rest."

"Why me?"

"The ritual is bound to your family line. You won't be blocked by the barrier around the altar."

"Oh." Blair rolled her eyes. "That's why they're trying to kill me. I can shut them down."

She exhaled hard. "Okay. Fine. Let's go."

"She's not the last person who can breach the barrier." I rubbed my chin. "Nigel said patriarchs from multiple families participated. But only he and someone named Edison had any real skill with the occult."

"Edison Wakefield," said Anna—aka Darth Grandmother—while gliding like a wraith into the room.

The name sent a chill down my spine, mostly because Nigel mentioned him. "Let me guess. He's a vampire now… and older than Remington."

Anna Bradbury smiled at me like a teacher proud of the idiot student for finally getting a math problem right. "Edison is Remington's father. He is the patriarch."

"It is highly likely he instantly became a vampire the moment he completed the ritual," said Sophia. "Whether or not he expected that result, I cannot say."

"Damn. The articles I read only referred to him and his brother as being the first Wake-fields to arrive in Shadow Pines—when it had been untouched ground. There's a *father* now?" I bowed my head. "I had a feeling we'd run into an even older, meaner vampire than Remington. Just *knew* it."

"It is highly unlikely that Edison would be

willing to disrupt the ritual as doing so would destroy him, too," said Anna. "It may be possible that a Farrington can do it, but I wouldn't trust them. They would either fight you all the way or deliberately damage the wrong focus."

"I said I'll do it." Blair raised a hand.

"Wait, are we really standing around here planning to drag a little girl straight into the heart of vampire town?" I asked.

Blair shrugged. "Technically, I used to live there. Not such a big deal."

"Have you ever seen Edison?" Crystal bit her lip.

"No. But Remington sometimes talked about him. I don't know if he's still around."

Sophia squeezed Blair hard enough that she gurgled. "I don't want her to go back to that place, but she's the only one who can disrupt the source of all of this. By breaking one object —the right object—she has a real chance to free Shadow Pines from the vampire invasion."

"Except for any who are not descendants of Edison," said Anna. "Any vampires not created by the ritual or sired by those who were created by that ritual will only be weakened by its absence."

Damn, it was sure weird to see Darth Grandmother with a facial expression other than severe disapproval. The old one looked genuinely worried.

"Can we rest?" asked Crystal. "Go tomorrow afternoon after some sleep?"

Sophia nodded. "Sure, honey. But, the ritual can only be broken at night. Doing it while the sun is up could have unpredictable results if it worked at all."

"The most likely outcome of interfering with it during the day is that the dark power well will close, but neither Edison nor any of his progeny will be destroyed," said Anna. "It would mean you'd have to track them all down. Also, they could continue to reproduce, cursing others."

Crystal glanced at her phone. "It's only a few minutes past eleven. Not that late. Screw it. Let's get this over with."

Aaron moaned. "I've been awake for more than twenty-four hours straight." He took a few deep breaths. "But, giving them more time to prepare is not a good idea, I agree. Okay. Fine. Not the first time I had to operate on no sleep. Just like the Army. I can do this." He pulled himself upright.

Sophia stood… and proceeded to get into an argument with Crystal and Anna. She wanted to go with us to protect Blair, but despite being a witch, every bit of magic she could do took hours to invoke and would be useless if a vampire pounced on her. Crystal and Anna wanted her to stay here and be safe.

Honestly, Blair should stay here and be safe, too. I didn't really want to bring a ten-year-old into a dangerous situation, but the plan didn't exactly involve taking the kid to Fallujah, merely the house she'd lived in her whole life. Even Sophia, who'd become as attached to this girl as she'd been to any of her daughters, said she was our best chance at succeeding. Blair agreed with the plan, but children had about as much foresight and concern over consequences as a beered up hillbilly yelling 'hey, Bubba, watch this.' Made for great fail videos on YouTube, but they usually ended up in a hos-pital.

In the 'pro' column, I didn't have complete trust in whatever anti-vampire wards theoretically existed on this property, so the safest place for the kid would be close enough to me that I could ask Mom Nature to ash any vampire trying to get close to her. Also, that kid had a chance to singlehandedly fix the town's vampire problem merely by taking one little object off a table in a basement. It wasn't like we needed to ask a ten-year-old to swordfight an elder vampire. Moving one... candle? Skull? Easy. We had to at least try.

Everything about this felt like a bad idea, but we didn't have any real choice.

Chapter Twenty-One
Harrowing

We headed outside to the police Tahoe.

"Kid, c'mere." Aaron opened the back door

"I'm Blair, not kid." She stopped short. "The last time a cop said that to me I almost died."

He rummaged in the back of the SUV for a moment, taking out a bulletproof vest. "Here."

Blair relaxed and approached him. He put the vest on her. It fit her a little big, but not too much so. She raised her arms so he could secure the Velcro straps around the sides.

"I don't think bullets are my biggest problem, but thanks," said Blair.

Aaron reached again into the SUV, grabbed one of the AK-47s we'd confiscated from the quarry, and offered it to her.

"Umm. That's not a good idea." Blair smiled, making no move to touch the weapon. "Max, I think you or Crystal should drive. He's so tired he thinks I'm a cop."

Aaron blinked, seemed to realize he tried to give a firearm to a ten-year-old, and exhaled. He put the rifle back in the truck, closed the rear hatch, and walked around to the passenger door. Crystal and I did rock-paper-scissors. She won, so I got in back with Blair.

The kid used the overhead light to examine a photo printout of the altar. "Which thing do I have to… eww. Is that a finger?"

"Yeah." I pointed at the bowl. "And blood. And an eyeball."

She stuck her tongue out, making a hissing kind of gagging sound.

"Heh. You saw a werewolf tear a guy into pieces, but that bothers you?"

Blair looked at me. "I don't remember that. Well, not the gory details. Too freaked out."

"Fair enough."

Crystal drove us out the gate, grimacing at me via the mirror.

"What? That's a 'this is a bad idea' face if I've ever seen one." I reached forward and squeezed her shoulder.

"Sorta. Just feels silly to leave a warded area

when every vampire in the city is going to try and come after us."

"Thank you for not saying 'kill Blair,'" said Blair.

Aaron turned in the seat to look back at me. "Are we really sure they're going to want her? I mean, she'd been stuck with vampires for years and they didn't touch her."

I scratched my head. "If they know that destroying that altar is going to pull the plug on every vampire who descended from the original ones the ritual made, they would, yeah. But, up until the other day, she wasn't the only one capable of doing it. All the Wakefield vampires had the ability, as did Nigel, and perhaps all the other family patriarchs who participated."

"Maybe not *all* the patriarchs." Blair offered a hopeful smile. "Nigel said only he and Edison had any real power. Maybe the others don't have the same kind of link to the ritual because they basically just stood there, doing nothing. At least, I don't *think* they do."

"I bet that's how Nigel controlled the vamps," said Crystal, while turning off their huge driveway to the road. "If they disobeyed him or got out of line, poof. All gone."

Crystal fidgeted. "That's probably what led to the Wakefields all going vampire... Nigel would have had one hell of a time going in there if they thought he meant to destroy them. The vamps were looking for a way off his leash. Minions turning on their master."

"Amazing they didn't tear him apart." I exhaled.

"If they did that, one of the others with the ability to breach that shield would have pulled the plug, so to speak." Crystal waved a hand about randomly. "I'm guessing. We are also assuming that the vampires all know this. We can assume Nigel did. That Edison Wakefield guy definitely knows—or knew—it. We've got vampires who are probably third, fourth, or even fifth generation descendants of the originals running around. If kids today don't even know what cassette tapes are, it's gotta be the same for vampires. Meaning, who cares about some dusty old ritual that sounds like a made up story... even to the vamps?"

"What's a cassette tape?" asked Blair.

Everyone laughed, except her.

"No, seriously. What is it?"

I rushed an explanation.

"Wow, you're old." She managed a feeble smile, clearly trying to joke.

"Not *that* old," I said. "Those things died out before even my time. I had CDs as a kid."

"What's a CD?" asked Blair.

I raspberried her.

"Okay, so what's the plan here?" asked Aaron.

Crystal eyed the side mirror as she drove. "Go to Wakefield Manor, bring Blair down to the altar room, and hope she can 'feel' which thing on that table is the primary focus."

"Sounds like we are relying on a lot of hope and luck to do this." Aaron whistled. "Great."

Crystal accelerated. "We've got a problem. Three cars are following us and they don't have any lights on."

I twisted around to look back, but couldn't see much in the dark as I lacked her low-light eyes.

"And guns," said Crystal.

Aaron leaned to his left, poking a button on the center console amid a cluster of buttons that civilian cars obviously didn't have.

Whoa! The road behind us lit up in the glare of floodlights mounted at the back end of the roof. As it did, I got a great look at the pale-as-hell face of two vampires inside a Dodge Charger less than a car length behind us. The surprised driver shielded his face with one arm —and didn't react when the road curved left a few seconds later. The undead bastard drove straight into the trees at about sixty miles per hour.

A tremendous *whump* came from the crash.

Crystal and Blair both jumped.

"We're not supposed to turn those lights on while driving," said Aaron in a slightly amused tone. "It could blind drivers. I think it might have a harsher effect on vampires who can see in the dark."

"Especially going from completely dark to sunlight brightness in an instant." Crystal laughed. "That hurt *my* eyes and the lights aren't even pointing in my direction."

The other two vehicles, an ordinary sedan and a pickup truck with oversized tires and a lift, had been far enough behind us that the floodlights hadn't completely blinded the vampires behind the wheel... but they did slow down.

"You sound entirely too pleased with yourself," I said.

"There are two kinds of motorists," said Aaron. "One type sees a police vehicle and stays way back, terrified of getting a ticket. The other type doesn't care and rides my ass. You don't know how tempted I've been to do that... so many times."

"What kind of idiot would tailgate a cop?" asked Crystal.

The crack of gunshots as a vampire in the back of the pickup started shooting at us.

Blair screamed and dove to the floor, curling

up. "Sorry!"

"For what?" I yelled, rolling my window down and hurling a lightning bolt at the truck. The bouncy ride messed with my aim, causing me to send the electricity into the hood. Flickering blue arcs wrapped around the pickup without much effect on it—or the vampires inside.

A dude in the truck bed did the funky chicken, though.

"For saying I didn't have to worry about being shot!" yelled Blair. "I jinxed us."

Another vampire stood up out of the sunroof on the sedan and opened fire on us with a handgun. Our power rear window slid down.

Aaron leaned through the seats, aimed his Sig at the pursuing car. "Plug your ears, kiddo."

An incoming bullet hit somewhere above me, probably the roof outside. Bet the guy aimed for the floodlights. Aaron squeezed off a few shots, smashing the windshield on the sedan and—I think—hitting the driver at least once. Much to my surprise, there *was* something louder than an angry, screaming Justine at midnight: a handgun going off inside a car. Yeah, I probably should have plugged my ears, too. *Yowie*.

Blair started shrieking and flailing, grabbing at her neck. "It burns!"

Oh shit! Had she been shot? Wait, burns?

She pulled the vest away from her chest, releasing an empty 9mm shell casing that had fallen from Aaron's Sig—which still hovered right above my head, firing.

"Dude!" I yelled.

Blair guarded her face and neck with her arms to avoid another piece of hot brass getting under her clothes.

The sedan revved and tried pulling up alongside us on the left. Loud honking zoomed by amid a screeching of tires. A car blurred past us going the other direction, forcing the vampire to swerve back into the lane behind us.

Since Aaron had opened the rear window, I didn't need to lean out the side door to send a lightning bolt into the sedan's hood, trying to kill the engine. Alas, my second attempt didn't do much but blacken the paint. Meanwhile, the guy standing in the sunroof finished reloading and took aim, but only squeezed off two shots before Aaron put a bullet into his groin.

That vampire collapsed forward over the roof, screaming. His gun slipped from his fingers, flew off the side of the hood, and disappeared into the night.

I cringed.

"Totally wasn't trying to do that," said Aaron, also reloading.

"Bullshit," I said in response to his tone. "You absolutely just shot him in the balls on purpose."

"Fine. I did. But it worked, didn't it?"

I chuckled. "He definitely dropped the gun."

"I said to myself, Aaron… what's a way that a bullet might bother a vampire?" He fired three shots, striking the driver with two of them, but the guy only appeared annoyed by it.

Behind us, the pickup swerved into the oncoming lane again, its engine roaring like one of those over-tuned rigs from a monster truck show as it pulled up alongside us.

"Go faster!" I yelled.

"We've got a child in the car!" Crystal glanced rapidly back and forth between the road ahead and the truck to our left.

I thought about trying to use wind, but didn't think I could sweep only one car off the road without taking us along for the ride. Lightning appeared to be my best bet, given its precision. People could survive real lightning strikes in their cars, so hitting the vehicles wouldn't work. I'd need to basically snipe the vampire directly.

The pickup side-bumped us. Crystal screamed as we almost fishtailed, but she regained control. As she did so, two vampires jumped from the pickup bed onto our roof. A mild curve in the road made me lean to the side. A vampire smashed in the window on the passenger rear door, sticking his arm (and gun) into the cabin. Still lying on the floor, Blair shrieked and kicked his arm upward, forcing his shot to go over my head.

Cripes, the bullet flicked my hair.

Aaron shot him near point blank in his upside-down face an instant before I covered him in fire.

Howling in agony, the vampire-turned-fireball fell off the right side of the Tahoe and went tumbling into ashy oblivion. His spinning body hit a tree and burst into a swirling shower of orange embers.

"Shiiiiit!" yelled Crystal.

It's never a good thing when the person behind the wheel of a car you're driving reck-lessly in yells that.

Before I could turn, a loud *wham* came from behind me (the oncoming lane). The pickup's engine roared louder, the pitch going even higher, basically redlined. I whirled to look, catching a smear of taillights. A sedan that had been going the other way had hit the pickup head-on, but slipped under its huge tires. The partially flattened wreck slid to a halt half off the side of the road—no sign of the pickup.

"Where'd the—?"

The pickup fell into view, landing upside down on the road, facing backward, skidding while throwing off a shower of sparks.

"They used that car as a jump ramp," rasped Crystal. "Did a backflip like fifteen feet in the air."

"I'd call that in, but I think we're the only functional police unit right now," said Aaron.

Crystal yelled, "If I stop to check on that other driver, the vamps are gonna ram us."

She reminded me we still had a vampire in a sedan chasing us. I faced the open back window, raising my arm. In the distance, the pickup exploded in a fireball. For a fleeting instant, that blast illuminated a person—a mortal person— standing on the road by the other crashed car. Whew. If they made it out of the car on their own, they couldn't be *that* hurt. They hadn't experienced a head-on collision as much as being run over.

I concentrated on projecting lightning into the driver of the sedan. A brilliant jag of electricity connected my palm to his face for a tenth of a second, making the floodlights seem weak by comparison. The vampire exploded into ashes. With no weight on the gas pedal, the car gradually began to lose speed.

"Flying Dutchman behind us."

"What?" blurted Crystal.

"Driverless car."

She kept us going relatively fast until the next bend in the road sent the empty vehicle into a ditch.

"Looks like that's all of them," said Aaron.

Blair poked me in the leg, pointed up at the roof, and held up one finger.

"Yeah," I replied, then repeated the gesture for Aaron to see.

He nodded, then tapped Crystal on the arm, mouthing 'one more on the roof.'

Aaron turned off the rear-facing floodlights.

Not quite two minutes later, Crystal hit the brakes hard, swerving in a skidding turn onto the private driveway that led to Wakefield Manor. Unfortunately, the abrupt maneuver didn't dislodge the vampire from the roof. One had to be up there. Two vampires had left from the bed of their pickup truck, but only one attempted to lean in our window and shoot us. That meant we definitely still had one on our roof... unless he'd fallen off when no one noticed. Better to assume the worst.

Crystal attacked the curvy, picturesque driveway like she tried to set a motor speedway time record and didn't much care if we plowed into a tree. Aaron grabbed the roof handle to hold on. Fortunately, Crystal managed to keep us on the road without flipping the SUV over or hitting anything. Once we reached the courtyard in front of the manor, she stomped on the brakes.

A man sailed forward from the roof, glanced off the hood, and hit the ground in front of the Tahoe.

"Well, that's one way dislodge a hitch-hiker," I said.

"Whew." Crystal exhaled. "We made it. Wow. There's nothing here. I expected we'd be charging into an army."

I opened the door on my side, jumped out, and raised my arm. "Maybe they didn't expect us to make it here alive."

The vampire who'd been roof surfing sprang to his feet and charged—right into elemental fire. Shrieking, he whirled around and raced toward the fountain, doing a perfect impression of The Human Torch. Impressively, he survived long enough to jump into the water and put himself out.

Crystal, Aaron, and Blair emerged from the Tahoe. We gathered in front of it, eyeing the giant house. Moaning, a charred, mostly skinless horror started to drag himself out of the water, saw me, and went back under. I probably could have commanded the water out of my way, but why bother.

It conducted electricity.

One lightning bolt finished him off.

"If it keeps up this way," said Aaron, "we're not going to need to do anything here. You'll have killed them all before we get to the house."

Crystal laughed. "If only."

We walked around the fountain, approaching the house.

"I don't like this place," said Blair.

The front doors swung open, shoved by a man in his late forties. Short, black hair framed a hard face that looked like it belonged on a cowboy from an old Western movie, the one that usually wore the black hat and shot innocent people for no good reason. He didn't have riding leathers or six-shooters, rather a shiny grey suit and a patch over his left eye. A dozen or so other vampires, mostly men, emerged from the house behind him.

Ever since Mom Nature gave me her gift, I'd possessed the ability to recognize vampires on sight. Well, mostly by smell, but also by an innate need to destroy them. And I had that innate need now. Eyepatch Guy gave me that feeling too, but also a healthy dose of dread. Dammit. When we took out Remington Wakefield, I had the distinct feeling an even older vampire pulled the strings. Pretty sure we'd just found him.

Sometimes, I hated being right.

"Uh oh," said Aaron.

"Who's that?" whispered Crystal.

Blair half hid behind me. "That's great grandpa Edison. He's a vampire."

I rolled my head around to crack my neck. "Yeah. Kinda had that feeling already."

"He looks upset." Aaron glanced down at his shotgun, seemed to grip it a little tighter.

"Yeah," I said. "Kinda had that feeling, too."

Chapter Twenty-Two
Unleashed

Crystal put a hand under my chin and pulled my head toward her, staring into my eyes. "Sorry, Max."

For an instant, my mind exploded in panic that I'd been betrayed… but an overwhelming need filled me, a desire to do whatever the most beautiful woman in the world wanted me to do. Nothing else mattered at all but making her happy.

"Let's kill some vampires," whispered Crystal, right before kissing me deeply.

"Gladly," I said, in a starry voice. "Anything you want."

"Don't hold back, Max." Crystal kept staring into my eyes as she pulled away. "I want these vampires gone and Blair mustn't be hurt."

Her desires became my desires. I'd happily dive in front of a freight train if it would make her smile. *Don't hold back, Max*. I faced Edison and the other vampires coming out of the house. Snarling, I made a grabbing gesture at the air, pulling at elemental earth energy with every ounce of power and desire I could summon.

Don't hold back, Max, whispered Crystal at the back of my mind.

The world trembled.

Okay, perhaps not the *entire* world, but my earthquake had enough *oomph* to knock several vampires, and Aaron, on their asses. Heeding my command, a towering mass of stone rose into the air, forming a humanoid shape covered in dirt, moss, and roots. Two glowing green energy spots approximated eyes, floating in front of a boulder serving as its head. I'd created an earth elemental half again taller than a person. The sight of it gave the vampires, even Edison, pause.

I was still holding back. Crystal would be upset.

"Kill them all. Except the child," said Edison. "She needs to go to her room. Forever."

The vampires rushed at us.

I want these vampires gone, said Crystal's

voice in my mind.

Arms stretched to the sky, I called out with no hesitation whatsoever, no fear of what possible harm it could do to me, and beckoned elemental air energy. Two bolts of lightning fell from the heavens into my hands, riding down my body with a searing hot charge that invigorated me like ten *pots* of coffee laced with high grade cocaine. I sent the lightning down my legs to the ground and forward, streaking among the vampires' ranks. Three of them exploded into ash clouds instantly.

When the two lightning bolts crashed into each other, they burst upward, forming into a crackling cloud. Sapphire-blue arcs snapped in flashes within a hanging mist. Two pale blue spots near the top gave the appearance of eyes.

Edison turned into a blur. One second he's thirty feet away, the next, his hand is around my throat and I'm off the ground. A grip like a forklift started to crush my throat, but he vanished the instant a low, grinding roar came from the earth elemental. Its massive stony fist punished the ground in front of me where Edison no longer stood.

Blair screamed.

A vampire had grabbed her by the bullet-proof vest, lifting her up over her shoulder.

Aaron, the closest one of us to her, point-blanked him with a shotgun to the back of the head… detonating his skull into a rain of gore. Fortunately, Blair, being bent over his shoulder, didn't see it. He collapsed forward, dumping her out on all fours behind him.

The air elemental threw windblasts and lightning bolts at the vampires, occupying the bulk of their number. Three closed in on Crystal while two rushed at Aaron. Apparently, my giant lightning display worried the vampires enough that only Edison had the balls to get close to me.

… want these vampires gone and Blair mustn't be hurt, said Crystal's voice in my thoughts.

She'd be *so* happy if I protected the kid. I had to protect the child.

Edison came out of nowhere and grabbed me from behind, but disappeared again as the earth elemental reached for him. I raised my hands in a lifting motion. A dome of eight-inch-thick stone rose up from the earth and engulfed Blair like a spider trapped under a cereal bowl. It didn't give her much room to move, but nothing short of high explosives could touch her for the time being.

A loud *splat* happened rather close behind me.

I spun, finding two stocking-covered legs

lying on the ground, a pink mini skirt, and an enormous swath of gore where a body had ceased existing from the waist up. The earth elemental had clobbered one of the younger vampires, bursting her like a ketchup packet. Pretty sure her entire torso had liquefied, while the arms and head simply vanished. Seconds later, the legs melted into ashes.

Normally, severe blunt impact wouldn't destroy a vampire. It had to be due to the natural energy suffusing that elemental. I didn't hold back, which should make Crystal really happy with me. Grinning, I looked around for Edison. He'd vanished again. Crystal had her hands full with a three on one fight. The two that went after Aaron dragged him to the ground.

Aww, shit.

I commanded the earth elemental to go help Crystal. Expecting Edison to come after me once my protector walked away, I pulled earth magic into my body, hardening my skin to stone armor, then threw a lightning bolt at a leather jacket punk moving in to bite Aaron. The thunderclap set off a *boom* that triggered a dozen car alarms among the expensive sedans parked around us. For the first time since I'd learned how to throw lightning, using the magic kinda burned my fingers. Still, I didn't hold back, pouring more energy into it than ever before.

The vampire popped like a soap bubble.

An electrical explosion on the ground beneath him flung Aaron one way, the remaining vampire another. A woman's scream came from way overhead. I glanced up briefly at a flailing vampiress in an evening gown, her glowing red eyes wide with terror. From the look of it, the air elemental had wind-blasted her like 200 feet straight up.

Edison clobbered me from behind.

In an instant, my view of the fight became a close-up view of driveway pavement.

The elder vampire's angry grunt came from way too close behind me.

I pushed myself up onto my side, glancing back at him shaking his apparently broken hand. The air elemental let off another lightning strike and accompanying thunderclap… as well as a satisfying *splat*. Edison sneered at me, then kicked me in the gut.

I landed about thirty feet away, stuck headfirst through the side of a Land Rover. Even with my stone skin, I'm pretty sure that knocked me out for a few seconds, but it felt like an instant. I extricated myself, the weight of my rock armor bending the metal of the door, and fell in a heap on the pavement.

The earth elemental grabbed a male vampire off Crystal, raising him up over its head and hurling him down. He didn't pop on impact, but the wet slap his body made sounded exquisitely painful. Doubtful he felt much pain since the elemental stomped on his head a second later, crushing it.

Edison blurred up behind Crystal and grabbed her, mouth open.

I raised a finger, about to advise him against biting her, but held my tongue.

He evidently realized what she was, hesitating without sinking his fangs into her neck. Again, the earth elemental emitted a long, low groaning roar. Edison disappeared in a streak of blur an instant before the elemental's stone fist smashed the courtyard, cracking it.

The air elemental threw lightning at the last two vampires in the main group, knocking them both to the ground, twitching. That woman in the evening gown, now a bloody mess, dragged herself away across the pavement in a series of short pulls, only her left arm moving. I rose to my feet and finished her off with a stream of flames.

Edison grabbed me again, but this time, the air elemental jolted him with a rapid three-strike of lightning. My little—okay, not so little—cloud buddy didn't have arms or legs, so the sparks emanated from the core of its misty form.

Surprised by the attack from behind, Edison stood there twitching, his remaining eye bulging from the effort he exerted to fight off the momentary paralysis. He glared into my soul, but I saw only a desperate old man who couldn't handle losing control of a situation. With Crystal's encouragement not to hold back echoing in my thoughts, I blasted Edison with fire, holding a flamethrower stream on him in a continuous burn.

The air elemental zapped him again.

He swooned down to one knee, roaring, reaching up past the rushing fire at me, fingernails sprouting to four-inch-long claws. Not sure why, but the sight of him basking in my flames without combusting didn't bother me at all. Like Remington, he'd be able to resist for some time before he ran out of power.

Again, the air elemental zapped him.

Crystal rushed over and hacked at him. He ducked, scrambling to the side and regaining his footing. I pivoted, swinging my arms to the left, keeping the fire stream on him as best I could. Resisting the flames dulled his power enough that he no longer moved like a movie on extreme fast forward. Crystal stepped into another swing. Again, he leaned back.

Blam.

Several grey spots appeared on Edison's face, flattened shotgun pellets. Not one of them penetrated his skin. He backpedaled, a look of fear in his eye. I'm sure he hadn't been genuinely frightened of anything in quite a long time.

Point for Mom Nature.

Crystal caught him in the throat with her sword, but the cut barely broke skin.

The air elemental nailed Edison with another lightning bolt that set off a concussion wave strong enough to knock me over on my back and send Crystal flying a few feet. The fire that had been streaming from my hand for the past minute or so stopped.

Shit.

I scrambled to get back up before Edison, no longer using up so much concentration to resist fire, could run off. He tried to dash away—and ran straight into the earth elemental's fist. The stone giant walloped him so hard he bounced off the ground in front of me. I tried to hit him with fire, but the old vampire jumped clear over me while I incinerated empty pavement.

Blam!

A force like a strong punch hit me in the back.

Aaron pumped the shotgun and fed me

another shell. The pellets didn't break the stone armor, but it did hurt like a dozen bee stings at once.

"Whoa, Aaron! What are you doing?" Except I saw it in his eyes... he clearly wasn't himself. Shit.

Edison pounced on Crystal, swooping around behind her. He grabbed her right wrist in one hand, the end of her sword in the other, and pulled the blade back against the front of her throat, glaring at me.

Blam!

Aaron shot me again. Damn mind-controlling undead bastards. Okay, now I was getting pissed.

"Don't think I'm going to die so eas—" began Edison.

I threw a lightning bolt over Crystal's shoulder into his face.

The thunderclap hurled Crystal forward onto her chest; Edison flew backward, landing flat and sliding. Snarling, I brought my hands together and commanded every ounce of elemental air I could into a lightning bolt as thick as a firehose. The painfully bright arc hit the elder vampire in the chest, splitting into five smaller branches following his arms, legs, and head to the ground. My fingers burned, but I kept pushing.

The air elemental dissolved into raw energy that flowed into me, then down the lightning bolt into Edison's body. The earth elemental collapsed, also giving me back its energy.

Roaring, Edison started to sit up, glaring at me with his one remaining eye. He reached toward me, struggling to sit up. Screaming in anger and determination, I kept pouring power into the arc connecting my hand to his chest.

Two seconds later, he exploded.

For an instant, only a char-blackened skeleton remained of him, then that, too, burst into an oblivion of ash particles. Spent, I swooned to my knees, the stone armor fading away. My fingers had gone red like I'd stuck them in boiling water, but I didn't care.

Crystal would be happy. So happy...

"Aww, shit. Sorry." Aaron's eyelids fluttered. "He made me shoot you."

"Don't worry about it. I had armor."

"You put a lightning bolt inches past my face," said Crystal.

"Yeah, I did. You told me not to hold back."

She leapt to her feet. "That's not what I meant!"

"Whoa. Did I really just make living creatures out of elemental magic?"

"You did. And it was pretty epic." Crystal took my hand, squeezed. Guess she forgave me for nearly hitting her with lightning.

"Guess I *had* been holding back." I squeezed her hand.

Blair tried to shout something, but her voice couldn't pierce the protective dome of rock surrounding her, only reaching my ears as an indecipherable murmur.

I commanded the stone to open. The bubble split apart at the middle, widening like a huge eyelid and sinking back into the earth.

The kid ran over and did her best to loom menacingly while glowering at me. "Why did you trap me in a tiny little space like that?!"

"To keep the vampires off you."

For a moment, the child appeared close to punching me in the head, but she ended up hugging me instead. Guess she preferred a mild case of claustrophobia to being carried off by the undead. Go figure.

"Are you okay?" asked Crystal.

"Little sore. But I'll live."

"I was asking Blair, you goof."

"Oh, right."

"I'm fine now," said the girl, this time hugging Crystal. "But you're hurt."

Crystal rubbed a few claw slashes on her side and arm. "Nothing that won't heal in an hour or two. How about you, Aaron? You okay?"

"I can't tell. I'm so damn exhausted right now, I wouldn't feel pain if I *had* been hurt." He whistled.

"Hey, holy crap! You blew up Edison." Blair kicked at the ashes. "Are we done? Didn't killing him destroy all the other ones?"

"Afraid not." I sighed. "Though that would be nice. Once the curse is permanent, killing the sire doesn't destroy the offspring. We'd need to break the ritual to set off any kind of domino effect. That's assuming Sophia's right about that."

"Oh." Blair frowned. "What if I can't tell which thing is the primary focus? I'm not a witch."

I drew my foot back to kick the dust out of spite, but ended up staring at a flaming eye patch atop the pile of ashes that used to be Edison Wakefield.

Son of a bitch.

Chapter Twenty-Three
So Totally Gross

Crystal looked down at herself, cringed, and plucked a stray vampire claw out of her left thigh.

"Why did you apologize to me earlier?" I asked. "Before the fight with Edison?"

She flicked the claw aside and smiled. "Because I had to charm you."

"Huh? Why?" I blinked at her. "I was going to fight that guy anyway, and I damn sure had no intention to let them hurt Blair."

Crystal leaned closer, nearly kissing me. "Because, Max, if I didn't charm you, Edison would have. At his age, he could take control of humans from merely looking at them. He had

Aaron for most of that fight, but the idiot vampires with him didn't realize that. My charm powers only work on most men, but it's stronger than a vampire's. Then again, I can't compel people to do obviously suicidal things, but the vampires can."

"Ahh. That makes sense."

We stared at each other in silence for a few seconds.

"Umm, guys? Remember when I asked if killing Edison would destroy all the other vampires?" asked Blair in a quivering voice. "I think I figured out the answer."

I glanced at her. "Didn't we already explain that?"

She pointed.

The three of us turned to look in that direction.

A group of roughly a hundred vampires dressed in everything from sweat pants to punk clothing to expensive designer duds swarmed onto the grounds. Some got out of cars, a few motorcycles, and a surprising amount appeared to have walked here. Even if I had it in me to call another elemental—which I doubted—the vamps would swarm us before it could deal with them all.

"Inside!" shouted Aaron.

Crystal and I both grabbed Blair's hands

before sprinting across the remainder of the courtyard and into Wakefield Manor. Aaron waited for us to all go by before he slammed and locked the front door. We dashed into the hallway that led to the kitchen, then raced down the stairs down to the basement. I expected more vampires in our way, left behind to guard Remington's personal chamber, but it appeared that Edison had been overconfident and never expected we'd get past him.

Honestly, that probably would've been a far more brutal beating if Crystal hadn't charmed me not to hold back. I felt like a character from some old Kung Fu movie briefly having access to the powers of his inner chi without limit.

The smashing down of the front door and breaking of windows upstairs lit a fire under us. We sprinted across the vampires' sleeping area to Remington's space. Someone had closed the secret bookshelf door, but it didn't take us long to find the special cherub wing and open it. After we ducked into the ritual chamber, Aaron pulled the bookshelf closed, then braced himself against it as if that would help hold back an army of undead.

"You're pushing against a door that opens outward…?" I blinked at him. "What's that supposed to accomplish?"

"Oh, duh." He stepped away and spun to

face it, raising his shotgun. "Let's hope they don't know about the bookshelf."

I put an arm around Blair and walked her over to the altar, pointing at the bowl of blood with its disgusting floating bits. "It's the eyeball."

"Seriously?" She scrunched up her nose. "Nothing feels weird to me. But... I mean, this entire situation feels weird to me. I mean the items. Ugh. Okay."

The kid started to reach for it, her hand going past the barrier as if it didn't exist.

"Wait!" shouted Crystal.

Blair yelped, and jumped back as if she'd burned her fingers. "What!?"

Crystal grabbed my arm. "How do you know it's the eyeball? Shouldn't you let her get a feel for the stuff?"

I tapped my left eyebrow. "Edison. Eye-patch. The eyeball floating in the blood is brown, just like his. That has to be *his* eye. The man who enacted the ritual put his own eyeball into the spell. Great sacrifice for great power. That *has* to be the primary focus. Plus... eyes focus. Get it?"

"Well, most people in this country have brown eyes. It's not that compelling of an argument," said Crystal.

The clamor of a hundred vampires storming

into the sanctum outside grew louder.

"Think it through," I said. "And quickly."

"Hmm. The eyepatch, he cast the spell, yeah, okay. It's reasonable." Crystal nodded at Blair. "If nothing else, you know, calls to you..."

Blair looked at the altar, studying the various objects.

Vampires began battering at the wall. They seemed to know where we'd gone, but not the location of the door or how to open it.

The kid's expression said 'screw it.' She thrust her hand into the bowl, grabbing the eyeball out of the blood. "Eww. This is so nasty. Am I supposed to say anything?"

"Hang on!" Crystal took her cell phone out.

"We don't have time to hang on," shouted Aaron.

The secret door wobbled as if the vamps, frustrated at not finding the latch, decided to simply tear the entire bookcase down.

"Mom? Does she have to speak any phrases?" Crystal listened, nodded, then waved at Blair. "Nope. Just destroy the focus object with the intention of closing the portal. Thanks, Mother."

Blair set the eyeball down on the altar table and picked up the dagger. Cringing, she held the disembodied eye steady with one hand while slicing the ornate blade through it to the stone, splitting the eyeball in half.

"Eww, there's like goop inside." Blair stepped back. "Did I do the right—?"

Boom.

Chapter Twenty-Four
Sacrifice

The explosion from the altar hurled Blair into me.

I more or less caught her, mostly since the blast wave had already knocked me off my feet so we kind of 'came together in midair' rather than me truly catching her. I hit the ground on my back, the kid on top of me, and slid into the wall. Aaron, already by the door, bounced off it and fell flat. Crystal managed to keep her balance, but staggered away with her arms raised to shield her face from a pelting of rocky shards.

"Eep!" said Blair.

Ouch. I sat up. The kid slipped down to sit

on the floor in front of me, gawking at a four-inch shard of rock wedged in the bulletproof vest along with a handful of much smaller ones. She grabbed the big piece in both hands and yanked it out.

"Oh, shit," I said, reaching for her.

"I'm okay. It didn't cut me." She rubbed the hole in the vest, then looked up from her chest. "Whoa. What is that?"

I followed her pointing finger with my gaze.

The stone altar had entirely disintegrated into a scattering of fragments. Instead of a little table at the middle of the room, I found myself gawking at a circular pool of indigo light bordered by a thin, shimmering haze of crimson. The surface rippled like water, giving off energy that prickled at my skin all over the facing side of my body. An immediate sense of dislike at the sensation filled me with the urge to destroy it, but I hadn't the first clue how to attack a puddle of light. Looks like Sophia had been wrong about the portal not being visible. Or… whatever Blair just did changed that.

"I have no damn idea." I stood, guiding Blair around behind me.

"You are not finished yet, Max Long," said a too-deep-to-be-human male voice.

Two bone spires rose up out of the portal, horns attached to the skull of a large human skeleton with exaggerated vampire-like fangs and long taloned fingers. The damn thing towered over me, my head not even up to its jawbone. Dark crimson flames filled its otherwise empty eye sockets.

Blair screamed. I nearly screamed too.

Aaron, wide-eyed, gripped his weapon and stood his ground.

The fiend pointed at me. "You have one final step if you desire to complete the mission the universe has chosen you for. Edison Wakefield committed his entire line to this bargain. To rescind the arrangement, the last surviving Wakefield must be sacrificed."

Blair clamped onto me, trembling.

"Go fuck yourself," I said. "Not happening."

The giant skeletal vampire took a step toward us, holding its scythe-handed arms out to either side. "Her soul was promised as payment for the power granted. This child was always intended as a sacrifice. Why else do you think they let her remain alive?"

I narrowed my eyes. "I don't give a rat's ass what anyone promised. I am not killing a little girl. Besides, I'm pretty sure you're full of shit. This girl's parents weren't even an itch in anyone's pants when Edison conducted this ritual. They couldn't have promised her in particular."

"Fool. You still think like a mortal. Those who wield this power see all futures." It took another step closer, its bony foot clattering.

"Nah. I think you're trying to trick me into killing her out of spite. She already destroyed your ritual."

A subtle change in the fiend's posture gave away irritation. *Hah. I'm right.* I shoved Blair into Crystal. "Get her out of here. Now!"

Crystal spun toward the still-closed book-shelf door. "We're blocked in! And there's a shitload of vampires out there."

"I know that. Teleport out! Now!"

The fiend rushed at them, raising a hand full of claws. I conjured a blast of fire, forcing the demon—or whatever it was—to flinch back.

Crystal lifted Blair off her feet and the two of them vanished. Their clothes, Crystal's bag, a bulletproof vest, and the dagger the child had still been holding hit the floor. I hoped she went somewhere safe—with privacy. Most likely, Crystal teleported them to her bedroom at the Bradbury estate. Childhood bedroom makes for a good instinctual safe place on short notice. At least, unless the house you grew up in burned to the ground... like mine had. My father loved reloading his own ammo, and he also loved smoking. Not the greatest combination doing both at the same time.

The creature roared in anger and charged at me. I'd done some reckless things in my life, but trying to brawl a giant vampire skeleton who had knives for hands *wasn't* going to be one of them. I dove to the left, hitting the floor. While scrambling back to my feet, I randomly grabbed the fancy knife. Only a ten-inch blade, but it looked important... and I'd watched enough movies to suspect an ornate dagger found on an evil magical altar might be required to—ooh, I think the blade is silver.

Yeah, this thing might actually come in handy.

Chapter Twenty-Five
Four Elements

The giant vampire skeleton caught me with a backhand swing a second after I stood upright. Felt like catching the side mirror of a passing semi-truck right in the cheek. The hit threw me across the chamber. I landed on my chest, but didn't stay still for long, jumping to the side an instant before its claws gouged the floor. Half on my back, I covered it in fire.

Aaron shot it in the skull. Thin trails of crimson fire spewed out of the pellet holes. Alas, it didn't appear too bothered by the modern weapon... only angered.

Roaring, it slashed down at my face.

Having nowhere to go, I tried a desperation

move: calling a shaft of rock up from the floor to block its huge arm. The hit broke the stone pillar, but stopped the claws from reaching me. I needed some distance, so I abandoned the fire stream and crawled up to a run, circling the shimmering indigo portal in the floor.

Sophia said the gateway only let energy pass through it, so maybe I could run across like solid ground even though it kinda looked like water. However, she also said the damn thing couldn't be seen and this giant ten-foot-wide energy pool was anything but invisible. She also never mentioned a freakin' thing about massive skeleton vampires, so no way was I gonna take a chance falling into an even worse nightmare than my present reality.

Aaron shot it twice more, not that the gun did any notable damage or slowed it down.

Once I stood on the other side of the energy pool, putting it between me and that giant bony horror. I pumped a lightning bolt into its chest. The *boom* of thunder proved obnoxiously loud in a confined room with stone walls. Aaron's mouth opened like he screamed while holding his ears, but I didn't hear anything. Electricity blackened a char mark on the creature's ribcage. Enraged, the fiend stormed around the portal to chase me. If that thing walked *around* rather than *across*, that meant people probably *could* fall in.

Thinking of the hours I'd spent shooting eight ball, maybe I could send this skeletal bastard into the center pocket. I conjured as much wind as possible, attempting to shove the monster into the hole. The fiend swiped at nothing, trying to seize hold of the air itself for support. Unfortunately, in a confined room with no windows, the strongest wind I could summon didn't shove it backward, merely slowed it.

Aaron rapidly unloaded the shotgun, firing five times as fast as he could pump it. Some of the fiend's ribs sprouted holes and a few bone chips went flying off in the gale. Sadly, the buckshot didn't appear to bother it much at all. As if noticing Aaron's existence for the first time, the giant pile of nope paused its slow walk toward me and swiveled to stare at him.

He dropped the empty shotgun and pulled his Sig, pointing it at me.

Aww, shit. Not again.

I dropped the wind and called on the earth, raising a phone-booth-sized enclosure of stone around Aaron. He fired three shots before the rock sealed him in. The first and third shots missed, but the second one hit me in the left arm a few inches below the shoulder.

"Fuck!" It felt like I'd been stabbed with a

searing hot icepick.

The creature leapt at me. I barely managed to duck the swipe going for my head, darting to the side while hurling fire backward at it. It chased me in a circle around the portal, running straight into my flamethrower effect like I spewed harmless cotton candy at it.

Shit! Why didn't this bony bastard burn? *Not* good.

For a moment, my chances of survival appeared better than they were since it couldn't quite catch me in a footrace. However, it jumped over the portal, crashing into me, carrying me across the chamber, and mushing me against the stone wall like a pissed off hockey player.

Blade-fingered hands grabbed me by the shoulders, lifting me up to eye level. Pain flared in the bullet hole, though panic kept me from noticing it too much. The crimson flames within its empty sockets brightened in anticipation as it opened its mouth to rip my throat out.

You know, for the most part, I considered myself to have a reasonable amount of courage. I'd gone into some dark alleys that most normal people would have avoided, even before I had 'magic.' However, being held immobile against a wall, my feet off the ground, by an enormous vampire skeleton with fire for eyes and six-inch fangs went beyond 'normal' scary.

Yeah, I screamed, and tried to poke it with the silver dagger. Though the blade sizzled on contact with bone, it had about as much success as attempting to cut down a tree with a butter-knife. I cringed away from the giant fangs as much as the wall allowed as it leaned in to bite me.

The blade of a sword burst out from its forehead, shattering bone and releasing a puff of crimson fire.

It froze, somehow managing to convey an expression of bewilderment with an inflexible, skeletal face. The blade withdrew, leaving a narrow slot hole surrounded by smaller cracks. Smoke wisped out of the slot. Fire in its right eye socket intensified, creating the effect of a raised eyebrow. It twisted to peer back at a sword floating in midair.

Thank you, Crystal!

Snickering to myself, I took advantage of its distraction to infuse my skin with elemental earth, hardening it to stone. Much to my disappointment, gaining a thousand pounds in four seconds didn't make the creature drop me.

The sword circled to the left.

"Aha. Your little succubus has come back to play." The skeleton sighed. "I do so loathe demons, especially half ones."

"She's not a demon. She's a fey."

"Even worse," said the skeleton in a tone like an irritated aristocrat. "Fey are the roaches of the outer planes. They get everywhere, and they're impossible to be rid of."

The sword flipped around and rose into a swing for the skeleton's neck. Alas, the monster threw me into Crystal, fouling her attack and knocking us both to the floor.

"Oof," barked Crystal. "You're freakin' heavy."

I couldn't think of anywhere else I'd rather be other than lying on top of her when she had nothing on... but this was *not* the time to be romantic. Besides, I couldn't feel a damn thing with my skin turned to stone. I braced my hands on the floor to take weight off her.

Her sword slid out from under me and floated into the air, as she undoubtedly rose to her feet. The vampire skeleton grabbed me by the right ankle, swung me around, and threw me into the far wall. If not for my stone armor, I'd likely have suffered a smashed skull, but the hit felt like I'd crashed into the wall of a padded cell. Still, disorienting. Damn this bastard was strong.

A *clank* came from behind me.

"Damnable wretch," muttered the vampire-skeleton-whatever-thing.

"Right back at ya, pal," said Crystal, and the

sword flew upward like she'd thrown it.

The creature spun, raking its claws through the air in a hard sideways slash—apparently it knew her throw-and-teleport-catch trick.

Crystal let out an *eep*, sounding far too close to it for my comfort. Fortunately, its claws hit nothing and the sword clattered to the floor. I nailed it in the back with another wind blast, shoving the fiend against the wall, holding it down so it couldn't chase her.

"Everything my minions saw, I saw. Throwing your blade away will not fool me. You have power that shall become mine."

Hmm. You know… that thing's eyes contained fire. Maybe burning it was a dumb idea. I shook my arms out to limber up, trying my damndest to ignore the burning from a bullet in my left shoulder. Calling upon the element of water, I hosed it down with an ice blast.

That made it bellow an anguished roar—and forget all about Crystal.

It rushed at me.

Crap. Hit a nerve.

Once again, I hauled ass in a circle around the portal like a little kid desperate to avoid a whooping. As expected, it leapt across the energy pool after a few times going around. Ready for that, I dove to the floor. The fiend crashed headfirst into the wall, breaking one of its horns. Crystal ran in swinging, landing four strikes on its back and right arm. Her blade chipped bone, but the cracks faded away in seconds. The holes the shotgun made had already vanished. It casually swatted her aside, not even using claws. Her sword flew halfway across the chamber, clanging to the floor mere inches from the portal. A second later, a smack like a huge raw steak being dropped on a stone countertop came from near the door. She appeared out of invisibility—a dazed look on her face—as she fell from the wall to the floor, cradling her bleeding nose.

Seeing her hurt infuriated me beyond reason. Shouting in anger, I showered it with another ice spray. The fiend raised its left arm to shield its face from the rain of elemental water. Undeterred, it stomped at me. Hoping my fury would batter down its defenses, I held my ground, trying to make this bastard thing into a snowman from hell.

Unfortunately, it did not succumb. I gazed up into its empty eye sockets, somewhat reassured by the apparent weakening of the fire burning within.

And that's when the bastard gave me a good approximation of what teleporting would feel like. One second I'm standing there, the next, I'm tongue-kissing the wall. And I've got a huge headache. Still growling—he sounded quite angry now—the skeletal vampire rushed after me, crossing the chamber in only three giant steps.

Crystal streaked—literally—by, two-handing her sword, chopping at its left femur in a strike that succeeded in cutting the leg off. The fiend toppled over sideways, crashing to the floor. On the way down, it raked its claws across my chest, shredding the hell out of my shirt. Nails on a chalkboard had nothing on the screech its talons made over my stony skin under said shredded shirt. Crystal kept running to get out of reach of any retaliation.

I resumed projecting a stream of ice at its back, sort of like a flamethrower, only cold. Paying little attention to me, it gave an irritated sigh while reattaching the severed limb. Damn. I decided to put some distance between us and hurried to the other side of the room.

"This damn thing is unstoppable," rasped Crystal. She stood hunched slightly forward, breathing hard, still holding her blade in both hands.

Figured I counted as scared shitless, since looking at her wearing nothing but dirt and blood didn't stir *any* impure thoughts at all. Not even any brief fantasy of what we might do later tonight... *if* we survived the next few minutes. Actually, not tonight. We'd both be far too tired. Tomorrow night.

Again, assuming we lived.

The skeletal vampire lunged at me once it finished reattaching its leg. Again and again, it smacked me with its giant clawed hands, swatting me around like a cat playing with a half-ton cotton ball. Hopefully, my stone armor wouldn't go away at a bad moment. If that thing hit me without it, I'd be ripped in multiple pieces from one shot. Crystal harassed it from behind, but it no longer even pretended to be worried about her sword. I guessed since it had slapped her in the face while she'd been invisible, she figured it could see her anyway and didn't bother disappearing again.

"Dagger!" I shouted. "It's silver."

The fiend tried not to react, but a momentary brightening of its eye fire betrayed its concern. She moved the sword to her left hand and ran to recover the knife from where it lay on the floor near Aaron's prison. At least that column protected him from the monster as much as it kept him from shooting me.

As soon as she picked the knife up, the vampire walloped me to the ground and whirled to charge at her. She let out a startled scream and threw the knife at it. The fiend raised an arm to block, the blade sticking between the two bones near the wrist. Smoke peeled away from where the edge made contact, but only for an instant before the creature tossed it aside. Again, it rushed at her. She backpedaled until she hit the wall—then teleported to the knife.

The charging vampire skeleton smashed headfirst into the wall for the second time tonight.

"We need a better plan," yelled Crystal. "Nothing is working!"

"I already told you what you needed to do." The skeleton turned to face us. "But you chose not to fulfill the promise."

"We're not killing a damn child!" I shouted.

Crystal stared at me with a look that said 'we are screwed.'

I refused to concede defeat. Mom Nature made me the agent of balance, right? That meant I had everything I needed at my fingertips. Guns didn't work. Her sword didn't bother it much. The knife might, but where did one stab a skeleton? This thing didn't have a heart or any other internal organs.

Think, Max, think. I had the power of the elements at my disposal.

I blinked. *Elements*. Not Element. Hmm.

My mind raced. It stomped toward us. Trying to slow it, I commanded a spire of rock to stab upward from the ground, smashing its way up through the concrete floor. The stalagmite punched the demon in the ribcage, knocking it back onto its bony ass. I raised two more stones to further break up the concrete and expose a wide area of raw earth. Unamused, the vampire fiend got back up and walked toward me as the stalagmites retreated back down.

As soon as it stepped into the exposed dirt, I combined water and earth energy, channeling them into the ground, making a deep mud bog. It sank to its hips, emitting an annoyed sigh. Before it could even start climbing out, I hardened the mud to solid stone, cementing it in the floor from the waist down.

Maybe I have to hit it with *everything*.

Realizing I'd quite thoroughly trapped it in place, the skeleton/demon/whatever howled and pounded at the massive stone cube partially encasing it. Hoping for an extra push of strength to my magic, I deliberately looked over at Crystal's bloody nose, becoming furious in an instant at this thing for hurting her. That fury channeled out of my arms into a lightning blast this bastard thing couldn't dodge. Crackling blue arcs wrapped around the bones, blackening them in places and lofting a burned meat stench in the air. I hit it with flames next, adding elemental air to the fire magic, intensifying the burn to white hot.

The beast screamed in anguish, flailing its arms in a futile effort to shield itself from the searing blast.

Crystal ran toward it; I stopped the fire so as not to burn her. She spiked the silver dagger into the top of its skull and teleported away less than a second before it would've shredded her with both clawed hands. The instant she cleared out of my way, I projected a beam of glowing blue ice.

Smoke poured from its eye sockets. Orange flames lapped out of the hole the dagger made.

"Die you big bony bastard!" I shouted, straining to throw every bit of power I could into the elemental water.

It reared its head back, screaming—then burst into a cloud of bone fragments and flame trails. The explosion paused, glinting bits of bone hanging in midair for a second or two before the debris collapsed inward, spiraling into the portal amid a roaring wind that made a jet aircraft seem quiet. As soon as the last traces disappeared into the energy well, the portal exploded in a conflagration of dark red fire.

The wall of burning hit me before I could even scream.

Chapter Twenty-Six
Balance

I'd expected to turn into that one little hamburger my father always managed to forget on the back of the grill. The one that sat there all damn day and ended up as a dry little hunk of meaty charcoal.

The flames hurt about as much as being burned alive ought to have hurt. Well, perhaps more so, since I didn't die or lose consciousness. It felt like an eternity of torment, but most likely had only lasted about five or six seconds.

Everything became quiet, still… and a bit chilly.

Wondering if I'd died, I patted myself down and discovered that while my body had survived the furnace intact, my clothing had not. My stone armor evidently decided to take a break, too. That explained the chill. I couldn't see a damn thing in the dark, at least until Crystal summoned this little ball of green light that floated around over her head. She still had blood smeared on her face and chest, but her nose no longer looked broken.

She ran over and hugged me.

I could think of a lot worse places to be than embracing her with nothing but sweat and dirt between us. The complete silence around us allowed me to relax enough to enjoy the moment. Seeing her alive and—mostly—unhurt choked me up. She didn't have stone armor. How the heck had she made it through that fire blast? The logic of what *should* have happened stole my voice. I could only hold her tight.

"I love you too, Max," whispered Crystal.

Right… she could feel people's emotions. Having no need to force myself to talk to tell her how I felt, we stood there in silence, holding each other for a while. Eventually, stinging pain made me curious enough to lean back and look down. I had a royal crapload of scratches on my chest, arms, and legs… plus a bullet hole in my left arm. Basically anywhere that damn thing raked its ridiculous talons at me managed to leave marks despite the stone. Fortunately, none looked worse than the wrath of a perturbed housecat.

"You're alive," I finally whispered into her ear.

"Yeah." She pulled her hair off her face and tucked it behind her ear, giving me an impish smile. "So are you. Can I make a small request?"

"Anything."

"I don't want to fight another one of… whatever the hell that was ever again."

"Yeah. Let's not. If we can avoid it." I looked her up and down. God, she was beautiful. She had a body that would've made Michelangelo fling himself off a cliff in frustration because he'd never be able to capture her on canvas or in stone properly. "How…"

"The fire? I'm half-succubus, remember? It takes more than fire to bother me."

I raised an eyebrow. "I thought you said you're not a demon."

She laughed. "Kidding. I teleported behind that stone column thing. Where did that come from, by the way?"

"Oh. The giant death monster mind-controlled Aaron. He's inside it. I didn't want to get shot, or have him be hurt." I pulled her closer to me. "You know, this feels like some kind of Adam and Eve sort of situation."

Crystal wagged her eyebrows at me. "Is that an offer of forbidden fruit?"

"Yes, but not here."

She laughed again. "Agreed. Are you really okay?"

"I'm fine, I swear. Claw marks sting a little, but that just tells me I'm alive. I think that bullet went straight through. Probably should get it looked at though. What did you do with Blair?"

"She's at your place borrowing one of your shirts. Probably asleep now."

I blinked. "You took her to *my* place instead of your estate?"

"Guess I feel safe there." She smiled. "First place that came to mind."

Thump. Thump. "Get me out of here," shouted Aaron, muted.

We turned at the same time, looking at the stone box. I lacked Crystal's indifference to nudity. Standing around in my birthday suit felt kinda awkward to me. Maybe the guy wouldn't mind waiting there a bit while I hunted down something to wear. Then again, he had the keys for the Tahoe. Or maybe Crystal did… in which case, they'd be a smoking melted ruin on the floor somewhere under the ashes of her clothing.

Dammit. At least the police truck had blankets in the back.

I raised my hand at the box and commanded the stone to open and sink back into the ground... except it didn't. Momentarily confused, I stared over my fingers at the box. Again, I concentrated on commanding the earth to move, but nothing happened.

"Umm."

Crystal looked over at me. "Why are you scared?"

"Not sure I'd call it *scared* as much as worried."

"Trust me. You're scared."

I swallowed. "It's not working."

"What isn't working?"

"Magic." I pointed both hands at the enclosure and tried to make the stone move by sheer force of willpower. Nada. "Shit... this isn't good. I poured so much power into that freakin' vampire skeleton I think my batteries are empty."

"Or it means you did it," said Crystal.

I turned my right hand palm up, lifting it a little the way I did when first noticing the wind obeyed me. Nothing. Not even a breeze.

"Don't be sad." Crystal hugged me again. "I think that means you did it."

"If anything got done, *we* did it." I stared at

my hands, feeling like a kid who got what he wanted at Christmas, then lost it two days later.

"Max," whispered Crystal, peering upward at the ceiling. "Do you feel that?"

"Right now, all I feel is useless. And your arms around me."

"Aww." She leaned up to kiss me on the cheek. "You are not useless. I mean, that super creepy feeling in the air that had been all over this manor house is gone."

She had a point. I no longer wanted to run the hell out of here as fast as possible. Of course, being naked, I didn't really want to go outside at all. As long as I stayed with Crystal, no one would notice me. Well, no one except women and men who had no interest in her.

"If your magic stopped working, that must mean you did it."

I squeezed her hand. "*We* did it. And did what exactly? Screw up?"

"No, dummy." She poked me in the side. "You said Nature gave you that power to bring back balance? Shadow Pines isn't eyeball deep in evil anymore." She sprouted a long, flexible tail, bringing the onyx spear head at the tip up to a little below her knee. "Only this deep."

She swatted me playfully on the butt with it. That tail is simultaneously creepy and cute. Thankfully, she can put it away wherever her wings go when she doesn't need it.

"Not a demon?"

"Nope. Fey." The tail vanished.

"Hey!" shouted Aaron from inside the box. "I'm still in here. Not possessed anymore. Let me out."

I walked over to the column. "We have a bit of a problem. It seems my magical abilities have decided to take a break. Do you have tools in the truck?"

"Yeah," shouted Aaron.

"Be right back." I headed for the door.

"Where are you going?" asked Crystal.

"To get a sledgehammer."

She raised both eyebrows. "You're going to walk outside naked?"

I shrugged. "It doesn't bother you."

"You're not an incubus, though. Humans are really uptight about going out in public while not wearing clothes."

I shoved the bookcase door open. "One, we don't have a choice. Two, no one is out there. Three, I don't want to spend the rest of my life in this pit. Four, there are blankets in the truck. Cops always have blankets."

The room outside, Remington's former chamber, had an inch-deep layer of ash all over the floor... not to mention about a hundred or so vampires' worth of clothing. Oh, that's convenient.

"We're in a giant manor house, Max. There's gotta be a sledgehammer in a shed somewhere… and all sorts of clothes upstairs."

"There's all sorts of clothes out here, too, if you don't mind shaking ashes out of them."

⚓

Chapter Twenty-Seven
Vacation

Two large explosions rocked my world in two days.

The first involved a lot of fire and quite a bit of discomfort. I enjoyed the second explosion much more. That one only went off inside my bedroom a day later. And yes, Crystal helped set it off. I think we laid there for about an hour before my brain stopped spinning enough to comprehend the world again. I felt like a cartoon character who had all their energy sucked out through a... straw.

She'd been hungry.

So, last night after I broke Aaron out of the pillar, we gave him a ride to his house, practically having to carry him inside to his bed. The poor guy was *exhausted.* Crystal followed us in a fancy Maserati GranTurismo that belonged to one of the Wakefields, so we could leave the police truck at Aaron's house. Technically, we didn't steal the Maz since it legally belonged to Blair—or would once all the estate crap went through. Not my style anyway. Far too fancy. Besides a car like that couldn't drive on half the roads around here without damaging itself. Shadow Pines is really the sort of place people need four wheel drive. I'd gone to the hospital to get the bullet wound cleaned up and stitched. It had been a through-and-through, so they didn't keep me too long. Worst part about it is being on antibiotics for a couple days. Well, that and the constant aching.

Blair spent the night at my place, already asleep on the couch when we'd gotten back.

We brought her home in the morning. Kid's taken a liking to me as something between a surrogate dad and a much older brother. Nothing like rescuing her from a colony of vampires and an eventual death sentence to get on a kid's good side, right?

Don Larson had snapped out of his mind control to the realization that his wife had been killed in front of him. Poor guy had no memory of abducting and planning to murder Blair, nor did he recall much of anything that happened after the vamps attacked him at night in his bedroom. He'd be taking a few weeks off to deal with his loss. Paul Ramirez handled it better. He'd lost a roommate, but they hadn't been best friends, only a couple guys splitting rent. Neither deputy knew how they ended up handcuffed to a radiator pipe in the old boarding house, but they'd eventually broken loose.

Except for a few hours earlier that afternoon where we'd visited Justine in the hospital, Crystal and I devoted the day to romantic stuff like scarfing down hamburgers and onion rings while watching cheesy vampire movies as well as talking on and off about living arrangements. She hinted at wanting me to move into the Bradbury estate. That sounded a little strange, like something out of medieval Europe where adult kids and their spouses lived all in the same house with their parents. I mean, the place had plenty of room. Not like we'd be crowded at all. It *would* feel kinda weird not living above my office, but… this place didn't exactly qualify as luxurious, or even average. Also, I'd vowed not to make the same mistakes I'd made with Justine all over again. Crystal, despite 'suggesting' it, appeared to genuinely want me to do it… so, I would.

We lay on the bed together after a marathon

lovemaking session, Crystal curled up at my side. It might've been four or five in the afternoon. Honestly, I hadn't looked at a clock in a while.

"You know… when they say a man's job is keeping his girl fed, I'm pretty sure this wasn't what they had in mind."

She laughed. "His girl or his dog?"

I laughed.

She snuggled closer. "You're not complaining, I hope."

"Not at all." I grinned like an idiot.

Crystal brushed her hand back and forth across my chest while talking randomly about her mother's adoption of Blair proceeding with remarkable speed through the local courthouse.

"Already? Nice. Great for them. Bribe a judge?"

She examined her fingernails. "No. She made a 'campaign donation.'"

I laughed. Or at least, emitted a wheezy sort of sound reminiscent of one. It'd be a while yet before I could laugh, or move. She drained me pretty good.

"Oh, Blair's developing an interest in mysticism."

"After all this, you'd think she'd want as little to do with weird stuff as possible."

Crystal chuckled. "She wants to protect

herself from things that go bump in the night. Mother's teaching her. Turns out the kid does have magical potential. She didn't even know."

"That's not going to end well." I squeezed her backside.

"Neither is that," she purred. "You're too tired to go again."

I looked up at the ceiling, folding one of my arms behind my head. "Sophia is going to train her how to become a witch?"

"Yes." Crystal sighed, her breath blowing warm over my skin.

"Hope that doesn't go wrong." I continued rubbing my free hand back and forth over her hip.

She emitted a soft moan, snuggling tighter to my side. "It shouldn't. My mother has a good sense about her."

On another note, my powers still didn't work. More and more, it seemed as though my batteries hadn't simply run out. Whatever Mom Nature had given me, I'd either used up or no longer needed. "I do really miss having magic. Oh, well. Suppose that just means I can pretend to be normal again." I stared into her eyes. "I'm really damn happy you didn't disappear, by the way."

"Don't worry about me. Nature didn't send me here for any specific purpose, nor did that dark portal have anything to do with my existence. Blame chaos and my mother committing a slight error with that ritual before I was born."

"I'm glad she made that error."

"More a miscalculation, really. Although she intended to summon an incubus, she never thought it would actually work. She also didn't expect it to want, umm, payment."

"You mean sex?"

"Yes."

"But how can she perform a spell like that without expecting it to work?"

"Do *you* believe in magic?"

"Yeah."

"I mean, before all this."

"Ahh. No. In that case, I wouldn't have. But your mother is a witch."

She snickered. "Yes. But even mystics don't believe everything they read. There's so much made up occultism out there it's often difficult to tell what's real and what isn't. I guess, think of it as finding a recipe online that looks like an impossible combination of ingredients that shouldn't go together, but it works."

"Makes sense. I think. Say, do you think I'll ever get my powers back?" I examined my fingers, frowned again, and let my hand fall back onto my stomach.

"I hope not."

"Not?" I blinked at her.

"If you got your powers back, that would mean things are way out of balance again."

When she put it like that... if having magic meant more vampires coming to Shadow Pines, I'd just as soon stay normal. That said, it really was going to feel strange to not hear about random 'animal attacks' going on in this town every few days. Hmm. How long would it take before the townspeople stopped being terrified to go camping or walk outside at night?

"Yeah. Better I remain normal, but if Mom Nature ever needed me again, I'd do it."

"You're a good man, Max. Better than I deserve. I still can't believe you really love me. Most guys just fall in lust with me."

"I'm the one that's in shock a girl like you even looked twice at a guy like me."

She kissed me on the lips—for a few minutes. Eventually, she leaned back and stared into my eyes. "You're the first man who ever looked at me and saw *me*, not only the outside."

"A man can't learn without making mistakes. I won't promise to be perfect, but I've done a lot of learning."

She grinned.

"So, no more magic," I said. "Guess it's back to ordinary cases for me."

Crystal raised both eyebrows. "You'd rather

be fighting vampires?"

"Nah. I didn't say that. Truth is, after the past few weeks, going back to the normal everyday grind is going to feel like a vacation. You know, Justine always told me I should take a vacation."

"When did she say that?"

"Eh, when she tried to convince me to stop investigating vampires. Didn't really come from her as much as the vampire controlling her. But... she raised a good point. Maybe we *should* take a vacation... once things settle."

"That sounds like a lovely idea."

We lay there in bed talking about the future, us probably moving into the estate. Eventually, going on a trip somewhere. I'd most likely keep working as a private investigator, though with the town losing so many sheriff's deputies and the number of missing persons cases around here poised to take a sharp drop, maybe I'd apply at the department.

According to Anna—Darth Grandmother—the Founding Families had flown into a bit of disarray as all the vampires they'd been relying on for spying, power plays, assassinations, and intimidation had disappeared. Half the Farrington family evaporated, literally. The Wakefields had already been wiped out except for Blair... and she even wanted to legally change her name to Bradbury.

The Anworths and Darceys barely noticed since neither of them had dealings with the undead. Crystal thought that might give them an advantage politically in the near term. Local gossip swirled with stories of random people bursting into dust. Depending on who one believed, three to as much as ten percent of the population here had spontaneously disintegrated.

So yeah... things around Shadow Pines looked to be on the way to relative normality, as normal as possible with witches and succubi running around, anyway. With Crystal, two witches, and a little girl on her way to becoming a witch in my life, it didn't seem likely to get boring any time soon.

Good thing I had that bottle of Jack in my desk.

Of course, it's not like anyone in Shadow Pines believed in things like vampires.

The End

This is also the end of the Max Long trilogy.
We hope you enjoyed it!

About J.R. Rain:

J.R. Rain is the international bestselling author of over seventy novels, including his popular Samantha Moon and Jim Knighthorse series. His books are published in five languages in twelve countries, and he has sold more than 3 million copies worldwide.

Please find him at: www.jrrain.com.

About Matthew S. Cox:

Originally from South Amboy NJ, **Matthew S. Cox** has been creating science fiction and fantasy worlds for most of his reasoning life. Since 1996, he has developed the "Divergent Fates" world, in which Division Zero, Virtual Immortality, The Awakened Series, The Harmony Paradox, and the Daughter of Mars series take place.

Matthew is an avid gamer, a recovered WoW addict, Gamemaster for two custom systems, and a fan of anime, British humour, and intellectual science fiction that questions the nature of reality, life, and what happens after it.

He is also fond of cats.

Please find him at: www.matthewcoxbooks.com

Made in the USA
Las Vegas, NV
03 September 2021